Transnational Repression and Extrajudicial Killings

Other Books of Related Interest

Opposing Viewpoints Series

Genocide
Human Trafficking
The New Censorship

At Issue Series

The Media's Influence on Society
Open Borders
Policing in America

Current Controversies Series

America's Role in a Changing World
Big Tech and Democracy
Reparations for Black Americans

> "Congress shall make no law … abridging the freedom of speech, or of the press."
>
> *First Amendment to the U.S. Constitution*

The basic foundation of our democracy is the First Amendment guarantee of freedom of expression. The Opposing Viewpoints series is dedicated to the concept of this basic freedom and the idea that it is more important to practice it than to enshrine it.

Transnational Repression and Extrajudicial Killings

Martin Gitlin, Book Editor

Published in 2025 by Greenhaven Publishing, LLC
2544 Clinton Street,
Buffalo NY 14224

First Edition

Articles in Greenhaven Publishing anthologies are often edited for length to meet page requirements. In addition, original titles of these works are changed to clearly present the main thesis and to explicitly indicate the author's opinion. Every effort is made to ensure that Greenhaven Publishing accurately reflects the original intent of the authors. Every effort has been made to trace the owners of the copyrighted material.

Cover image: boyphare/Shutterstock.com

Library of Congress CataloginginPublication Data

Names: Gitlin, Martin, editor.
Title: Transnational repression and extrajudicial killings / edited by Martin Gitlin.
Description: First edition. | Buffalo, NY : Greenhaven Publishing, 2025. | Series:
Opposing viewpoints | Includes bibliographical references and index.
Identifiers: ISBN 9781534509795 (pbk.) | ISBN 9781534509801 (library bound)
Subjects: LCSH: Transnationalism. | Transnationalism--Political aspects.| Political persecution--History--21st century. | Authoritarianism--21st century.Extrajudicial executions.
Classification: LCC JZ1320.T736 2025 | DDC 305.8--dc23

Manufactured in the United States of America

Website: http://greenhavenpublishing.com

Contents

Chapter 3: Are Extrajudicial Killings Common on the Global Stage?

Chapter 4: Can Transnational Repression and Extrajudicial Killings Be Punished and Prevented?

The Importance of Opposing Viewpoints

Perhaps every generation experiences a period in time in which the populace seems especially polarized, starkly divided on the important issues of the day and gravitating toward the far ends of the political spectrum and away from a consensus-facilitating middle ground. The world that today's students are growing up in and that they will soon enter into as active and engaged citizens is deeply fragmented in just this way. Issues relating to terrorism, immigration, women's rights, minority rights, race relations, health care, taxation, wealth and poverty, the environment, policing, military intervention, the proper role of government—in some ways, perennial issues that are freshly and uniquely urgent and vital with each new generation—are currently roiling the world.

If we are to foster a knowledgeable, responsible, active, and engaged citizenry among today's youth, we must provide them with the intellectual, interpretive, and critical-thinking tools and experience necessary to make sense of the world around them and of the all-important debates and arguments that inform it. After all, the outcome of these debates will in large measure determine the future course, prospects, and outcomes of the world and its peoples, particularly its youth. If they are to become successful members of society and productive and informed citizens, students need to learn how to evaluate the strengths and weaknesses of someone else's arguments, how to sift fact from opinion and fallacy, and how to test the relative merits and validity of their own opinions against the known facts and the best possible available information. The landmark series Opposing Viewpoints has been providing students with just such critical-thinking skills and exposure to the debates surrounding society's most urgent contemporary issues for many years, and it continues to serve this essential role with undiminished commitment, care, and rigor.

The key to the series's success in achieving its goal of sharpening students' critical-thinking and analytic skills resides in its title—

Opposing Viewpoints. In every intriguing, compelling, and engaging volume of this series, readers are presented with the widest possible spectrum of distinct viewpoints, expert opinions, and informed argumentation and commentary, supplied by some of today's leading academics, thinkers, analysts, politicians, policy makers, economists, activists, change agents, and advocates. Every opinion and argument anthologized here is presented objectively and accorded respect. There is no editorializing in any introductory text or in the arrangement and order of the pieces. No piece is included as a "straw man," an easy ideological target for cheap point-scoring. As wide and inclusive a range of viewpoints as possible is offered, with no privileging of one particular political ideology or cultural perspective over another. It is left to each individual reader to evaluate the relative merits of each argument—as they see it, and with the use of ever-growing critical-thinking skills—and grapple with their own assumptions, beliefs, and perspectives to determine how convincing or successful any given argument is and how the reader's own stance on the issue may be modified or altered in response to it.

This process is facilitated and supported by volume, chapter, and selection introductions that provide readers with the essential context they need to begin engaging with the spotlighted issues, with the debates surrounding them, and with their own perhaps shifting or nascent opinions on them. In addition, guided reading and discussion questions encourage readers to determine the authors' point of view and purpose, interrogate and analyze the various arguments and their rhetoric and structure, evaluate the arguments' strengths and weaknesses, test their claims against available facts and evidence, judge the validity of the reasoning, and bring into clearer, sharper focus the reader's own beliefs and conclusions and how they may differ from or align with those in the collection or those of their classmates.

Research has shown that reading comprehension skills improve dramatically when students are provided with compelling, intriguing, and relevant "discussable" texts. The subject matter of these collections could not be more compelling, intriguing, or urgently relevant to today's students and the world they are poised to inherit. The anthologized articles and the reading and discussion questions that are included with them also provide the basis for stimulating, lively, and passionate classroom debates. Students who are compelled to anticipate objections to their own argument and identify the flaws in those of an opponent read more carefully, think more critically, and steep themselves in relevant context, facts, and information more thoroughly. In short, using discussable text of the kind provided by every single volume in the Opposing Viewpoints series encourages close reading, facilitates reading comprehension, fosters research, strengthens critical thinking, and greatly enlivens and energizes classroom discussion and participation. The entire learning process is deepened, extended, and strengthened.

For all of these reasons, Opposing Viewpoints continues to be exactly the right resource at exactly the right time—when we most need to provide readers with the critical-thinking tools and skills that will not only serve them well in school but also in their careers and their daily lives as decision-making family members, community members, and citizens. This series encourages respectful engagement with and analysis of opposing viewpoints and fosters a resulting increase in the strength and rigor of one's own opinions and stances. As such, it helps make readers "future ready," and that readiness will pay rich dividends for the readers themselves, for the citizenry, for our society, and for the world at large.

Introduction

> *"The next phase in addressing the threat of transnational repression must ensure that America's own institutions and practices cannot be easily co-opted by authoritarian states seeking to harm political exiles and diasporas."*
>
> – *Freedom House*

It was October 2, 2018. Saudi journalist and dissident Jamal Khashoggi was ambushed while entering the Saudi consulate in Istanbul, Turkey. His dead body was found dismembered. The 15-member goon squad that murdered him had been sent by the Saudi government in a horrific case of extrajudicial killing. His final moments were captured in audio recordings and the transcripts were eventually made public.

The details were gruesome. But Khashoggi was not alone as a victim. His story simply gained the most media exposure, greatly because of what some considered to be a lukewarm response from the American government, which was perceived to care more about its relationship with Saudi Arabia than taking a moral stand against such brutality. The American government was even lambasted by some for its targeted killings of its enemies and claiming it did not fall under the same category.

It was eventually reported that Saudi leadership engaged in a wide-ranging effort to cover up the murder, even destroying evidence. More investigations revealed that the killing was premeditated and that some members of the hit team were closely connected to Mohammed bin Salman, the crown prince of Saudi

Arabia. That revelation had been suspected all along. But as time marched on through that decade and into the next one, it had become obvious that those who carried out extrajudicial killings cared little about world opinion, particularly since they suffered little or no retribution.

These pages will define, explain, and analyze extrajudicial killing while showing sides to various relevant arguments. It will also delve deeply into the proliferation of transnational repression, a more commonly carried-out form of oppression and suppression used mostly by authoritarian regimes to stifle the freedom of expression by those who have left their countries to seek those very freedoms.

Extrajudicial killing is the ultimate form of transnational repression. Every instance of both can be judged on its own merit and surrounding circumstances but, at least in free and democratic nations, one and all are considered morally wrong. The question then comes what can be done about it. Therein lies the problem. Sanctions are often placed on offending countries but those often prove ineffective. Military options are particularly dangerous when superpowers such as Russia and China are involved—and the latter is seen globally as among the most frequent wrongdoers.

This book examines many sides of both transnational repression and extrajudicial killing. It provides a historical perspective to give readers factual background information. Some viewpoints express strong opinions and causes and effects of these monsters on the global stage that have earned a stronger-than-ever spotlight. Also included among the pieces here are viewpoints on the best methods for containing or even stopping these practices.

What indeed is the answer? Does the United Nations have the power or even credibility to offer and carry out a solution? Do democratic nations such as the United States, supposedly a moral beacon to the oppressed throughout the world, have a responsibility to act, or is it in reality just another perpetrator of transnational repression and occasional extrajudicial killings? Is American history replete with such examples—in the past and today—considering the many lynchings that occurred during the Jim Crow era, the subjugation and murder of Native Americans in the 1800s, and highly publicized murders of Black men and women by overzealous police in the modern day? Or do those terrible transgressions not fall into the same category?

The digital age has in many ways shrunk the world and made transnational repression easier and far more common. Internet threats over social media intimidate, and the computer age gives hackers who seek to do harm vital information on where to locate victims and the ability to destroy lives online. That has vastly increased the number of incidents of transnational repression in the 21st century.

But what are the motivations? Should superpowers such as Russia and China really be threatened by a handful—or even a larger number—of dissidents who might speak unkindly about their regimes? Is punishment through transnational repression or even murder so tantalizing an option that it must be carried out? Or do the governments of those countries and others actually feel threatened by those whose lives they wish to ruin or perhaps end?

Opposing Viewpoints: Transnational Repression and Extrajudicial Killings features the writings of legal and political scholars, journalists, and those working with various relevant organizations and several different countries. They offer their studied opinions on these subjects. Their learned views come from many outlooks and backgrounds and are certainly varied. It is up to the readers to soak it all in and make their own assertions based on the knowledge and contentions offered in these pages.

Chapter 1

Is Transnational Repression Becoming More Common?

Chapter Preface

What is transnational repression? What are its forms? Why are authoritarian countries far more likely to practice it? What are their motivations? What are the outcomes? Do they feel a sense of free rein over their victims? Do they feel safe in carrying out such tactics? What is the future of transnational repression?

These are the questions asked and debated in this chapter. Some of the viewpoints that follow trace examples of transnational repression back centuries, though at that time it was a practice that had no name. But Chapter 1 delves more into forms of transnational repression and the nations that are most responsible. Most notable are those in the Middle East and China.

Some argue that places the problem into the laps of Western democracies who must respond to transnational repression, much of which takes place within their own borders as dissidents from and of countries with repressive governments flee to what they perceive as safer havens. How democracies that boast about their freedoms react will go a long way in determining how often and expansive such practices will prove to be in the future. Some authors of Chapter 1 viewpoints provide speculation based on past democratic government reactions.

An inability or unwillingness by the U.S. government to crack down on transnational repression inside its own country is the fodder for debate in this chapter as well. The charge is not that the American government practices such harmful acts on others but that it is not doing enough to stop other nations, largely because their relationships with those countries are more important than taking a moral stand. There is some merit to that mindset, especially in regard to superpowers Russia and China, because of tenuous international relationships.

Viewpoint 1

> *"China, which conducts the most comprehensive and sophisticated campaign of transnational repression, is responsible for 30 percent of the cases."*

Transnational Repression Is a Global Threat

Michael Abramowitz

The following viewpoint by Michael Abramowitz provides a starting point for discussions about transnational repression through commentary and statistical background. It cites the most blatant offenders and their targets and warns of its negative impact on freedom and the security of those who wish to practice free speech. Abramowitz points out that although transnational repression is not a new issue, it is becoming an increasingly larger problem. Michael Abramowitz is a former president of Freedom House, a non-partisan organization that aims to protect democracy.

As you read, consider the following questions:

1. Why are free and democratic nations not among those listed as the top perpetrators of transnational repression?
2. What suggestions are offered in this viewpoint about how to limit or halt transnational repression?

"Transnational Repression: A Global Threat to Rights and Security," by Michael Abramowitz, Freedom House, December 7, 2023. Reproduced with permission.

3. According to this viewpoint, what progress has been made in combating transnational repression?

Transnational repression occurs when states reach across borders to silence dissent from activists, journalists, and others living in exile. Perpetrator states do so using intimidation and violence. This issue presents a direct threat to rights and security around the world, including here in the United States, and will require a coordinated response from across the U.S. government and between the United States and other democratic governments.

From 2014 through 2022, Freedom House has collected information on 854 direct, physical incidents (assassination, kidnapping, assault, detention, or deportation) of transnational repression around the world, committed by 38 governments in 91 countries. During this time, 13 states have engaged in assassinations abroad, and 30 have conducted renditions.

These numbers are likely only the tip of the iceberg, as states also use indirect tactics to intimidate activists in exile, such as the use of spyware, surveillance, threats sent over social media or phone, or threats against family members back home (known as coercion by proxy).

The top five perpetrators in our assessment are China, Turkey, Tajikistan, Egypt, and Russia—while Turkmenistan, Uzbekistan, Iran, Belarus, and Rwanda round out the top 10. These 10 countries are responsible for 80 percent of the cases in our database. And China, which conducts the most comprehensive and sophisticated campaign of transnational repression, is responsible for 30 percent of the cases.

In the last several years, these countries have undertaken brazen measures to intimidate and silence their exiles and diasporas. One of the most famous cases in the United States involves the Iranian regime's plot to kidnap journalist and women's rights activist Masih Alinejad from her home in Brooklyn. When that didn't work, Iran attempted an assassination plot that was thankfully also unsuccessful. To this day, Alinejad lives under federal protection.

Just weeks ago, a group of activists were physically assaulted in San Francisco during the Asia Pacific Economic Cooperation (APEC) Summit while protesting human rights violations by Xi Jinping and the ruling Chinese Communist Party. In 2021, Belarusian officials called a fake bomb threat into a Ryanair flight from Greece to Lithuania, forcing an emergency landing in Minsk in order to apprehend a blogger critical of the ruling regime. Only 13 months ago, Emirati law enforcement arrested Egyptian American activist and former Egyptian army officer Sherif Osman based on a request from Egypt. Russian journalists Elena Kostyuchenko and Irina Babloyan were poisoned in late 2022, possibly in connection with their critical reporting on Russia's full-scale invasion of Ukraine. Throughout 2022, Tajikistan's government expanded its campaign of transnational repression against members of the Pamiri ethnic group, securing the extradition from Russia of outspoken Pamiri activists such as Oraz and Ramzi Vazirbekov.

This does not mean that only authoritarian governments are responsible for incidents of transnational repression. In September, Canadian Prime Minister Justin Trudeau announced that Canada's security services had intelligence linking "agents of the government of India" to the June murder of Sikh activist and Canadian citizen Hardeep Singh Nijjar in British Columbia. And on November 29, the Department of Justice alleged in an indictment that an Indian national in India was hired by an Indian government official to orchestrate the assassination of a U.S. citizen who is a Sikh activist.

An Old but Growing Problem

In some ways, transnational repression is a new term for an old problem. As long as states and leaders have seen themselves as threatened by dissent outside their borders, they have tried to control that dissent, and sometimes have resorted to coercion to do so. There are legions of historical examples, from the murder of Iranian exiles in Europe after the revolution to the car bomb murder of Orlando Letelier in Washington, DC, by Chilean government agents.

What has changed is the dynamic between those who leave and the states they leave behind, and with it the scale and scope of transnational repression. The increased scale of global migration has knit our world closer together as more people move across borders and build lives in different countries. It should also be recognized that more and more activists and journalists are being driven from their home communities by authoritarian powers closing down space for them to operate freely. In Russia alone, hundreds of journalists and activists have fled Vladimir Putin's crackdown, setting up operations to continue their work in Georgia, Armenia, Germany, Lithuania, and other countries in Europe and Eurasia, all while remaining politically engaged in their origin states.

Digital technology has enabled exiled individuals and groups to remain connected to their origin countries, posting on social media and messenger apps that reach people within milliseconds instead of arduously smuggling physical samizdat across borders. States, in turn, have gained instantaneous capabilities to surveil their overseas critics through social media monitoring and spyware. That surveillance all too often leads to concrete threats against those living in the diaspora.

One of the most recent and worrying developments is the extraterritorial repression of reporters. As the space for free media and dissent has closed in authoritarian countries, governments are increasingly reaching outward to target exiled journalists who continue to do their courageous work from abroad. Our new report released today, titled "A Light That Cannot Be Extinguished: Exiled Journalism and Transnational Repression," examines this issue more closely and describes the repressive toolkit used against target exiled journalists and media. At least 26 governments have targeted journalists, and 112 of the 854 cases in our database—13 percent of all cases—involved journalists.

Perpetrator states of transnational repression are innovating even as awareness of the problem in host countries grows. Moving forward, host governments and law enforcement must pay increasing attention to the role of diplomatic staff and proxy actors working on behalf of origin states to intimidate exiles. The aforementioned recently unsealed DOJ indictment alleging a murder-for-hire scheme organized by an Indian government employee against a Sikh activist in New York City points to the involvement of criminal associates in such plots. Additionally, foreign governments, such as that of China, may continue to seek out private investigators to co-opt host state institutions and more easily reach targeted individuals.

For too long, democracies have missed or allowed the actions of authoritarian countries inside their borders. Such a pattern of impunity has emboldened states to act abroad without fear of consequences.

A Global Threat to Rights and Security

When we see the Russian government for years get away with killing its opponents abroad in baroque schemes across Europe; when we see the murder of Jamal Khashoggi literally inside Saudi Arabia's Istanbul consulate go unpunished; when we see the Turkish government boast officially that it has kidnapped over 100 people from abroad without any consequence; when we see Rwanda kidnap regime critic Paul Rusesabagina off of a Dubai tarmac; when we see armed Iranian agents visiting the house of journalist Masih Alinejad in Brooklyn; when we see an Indian government agent plotting to murder a Sikh activist in New York City; we have a global problem. Transnational repression poses a threat to both rights and security and a challenge for both domestic and foreign policy.

The impact of transnational repression on targeted individuals is severe. People's physical safety is endangered, their travel is complicated, their houses are surveilled in the U.S. and elsewhere, they are harassed online and offline, and communication with family and friends living in the country of origin is fraught. Some people are cut off from their families entirely. Each individual incident of transnational repression produces ripple effects throughout the community, fostering an atmosphere of fear and suspicion among neighbors and compatriots.

Even when taking care to avoid being impacted by transnational repression, individuals may still face imprisonment and the possibility of deportation. To take one example, Idris Hasan, a Uyghur activist, has been in a Morocco prison for two-and-a-half years after he was detained upon arrival on the basis of a since invalidated Interpol notice requested by China. Hasan's detention in Casablanca was particularly unfortunate, as he had opted to flee Turkey due to the uptick in pressure from the Turkish government on outspoken Uyghurs.

The fundamental question is whether democratic societies can and will protect the rights of people inside our borders against such intimidation. The bet that autocrats are making is that we are not willing to bear the cost of doing so. We must prove them wrong.

Declaration of Principles to Combat Transnational Repression

The Declaration of Principles to Combat Transnational Repression calls upon democratic governments to acknowledge and commit to addressing the increasingly prevalent phenomenon of transnational repression, whereby states reach across borders to harm, intimidate, and silence journalists, activists, dissidents, and diaspora communities.

Transnational repression is a threat to democracy and human rights worldwide. It undermines the rule of law, imperils civil and political liberties, and spreads authoritarianism. Combatting transnational repression requires ending impunity for perpetrators, strengthening the resilience of democratic institutions, and protecting vulnerable groups and individuals.

Signatories of this Declaration of Principles hereby acknowledge transnational repression as an issue requiring urgent attention and response, and commit to working to address impunity, build resilience, and protect the vulnerable.

Specifically, signatories will strive to:

- Increase awareness of the threat of transnational repression for officials at the national and subnational levels, including border enforcement, immigration, cybersecurity, and law enforcement personnel, so officials are better able to recognize threats, appropriately respond to them, and assist victims as needed.
- Increase outreach to potential targets of transnational repression, in coordination with civil society, to alert potential targets to threats, inform them of their rights, and explain how they can report incidents.
- Establish clear procedures for the public to report to relevant domestic authorities attacks, threats, or harassment by foreign states or actors.
- Ensure that domestic laws provide officials with the authority and tools needed to apprehend and prosecute perpetrators of transnational repression.
- Ensure that human rights activists and civil society organizations have access to international forums where they can share their experiences and raise awareness of the threat of transnational repression.
- Publicly and privately call out perpetrators of transnational repression.
- Increase accountability for perpetrators of transnational repression through measures including targeted sanctions and diplomatic consequences.
- Press for increased transparency at the International Criminal Police Organization (Interpol), as well as reforms to domestic procedures for the use of Interpol notices where necessary to ensure such notices are not misused by authoritarian regimes to trick officials and officers of democratic governments into detaining regime critics at their behest.
- Take into account other countries' practices and histories of transnational repression when considering bilateral security agreements, extradition treaties, foreign aid, and information-sharing practices.

continued on next spread

- Impede, including through export controls and licensing restrictions, the misuse of surveillance technologies, including commercial spyware, for digital transnational repression, and impose strong domestic controls to prevent the misuse of such technologies.

This Declaration of Principles is an initiative of the Resisting Authoritarian Pressure cohort, which was established by Freedom House, the Lithuanian Ministry of Foreign Affairs, and the Alliance of Democracies during the Year of Action following the first Summit for Democracy in December 2021.

Government Endorsements

- Commonwealth of Australia
- Federal Republic of Germany
- Republic of Chile
- Republic of Estonia
- Republic of Kosovo
- Republic of Latvia
- Republic of Lithuania
- Slovak Republic
- United States of America

"Declaration of Principles to Combat Transnational Repression" by Freedom House.

Progress So Far

Transnational repression is part of a pattern of authoritarian powers seeking to globalize the repression they use to maintain control in their own societies. Thankfully, there has been strong, bipartisan interest in addressing this issue here in the United States and a growing interest from democracies in Europe and elsewhere.

The Biden administration has made addressing transnational repression a priority issue across agencies. We are pleased to see strong interagency coordination, and, as we understand it, increasing engagement between the executive branch and the Hill—something crucially important for an effective U.S. response.

Among the steps taken by the U.S. government: The Commerce Department has moved to rein in the use of American technology in the production of powerful commercial spyware, which is a crucial vector of transnational repression. The State and Treasury departments have sanctioned perpetrators of transnational repression. State has been holding trainings for diplomats, engaging with allies around the world, and coordinating emergency responses for diaspora communities and exiles abroad. The Department of Homeland Security has pursued outreach to vulnerable communities inside the U.S. The FBI has a dedicated stream of work on transnational repression, including a public web page, the issuance of several informational bulletins for targeted communities, and the ability for individuals to report transnational repression to the FBI hotline. And, we have seen the Department of Justice investigate and prosecute a growing number of cases of transnational repression plotted against U.S. persons, sending a powerful signal to perpetrators and their agents that these actions will be caught and punished.

There are also a number of bills pending in Congress, including some authored by members of this committee.

These are all important steps that we and others have encouraged, and we applaud these efforts. But more action is needed.

Recommendations for Congress

We urge Congress to strengthen the U.S. response to transnational repression and ensure the U.S. has the tools needed to protect those within our borders for years to come. There are three specific steps Congress can take.

1) Pass legislation to address gaps in the U.S. government's response to transnational repression. This includes codifying a definition of transnational repression, ensuring government officials who may encounter perpetrators or victims of transnational repression receive the training necessary to recognize and respond

to the problem, and strengthening sanctions authorities to make it easier to hold perpetrators accountable. The Transnational Repression Policy Act, which was introduced by Senators Merkley, Rubio, Cardin, and Hagerty, includes provisions in all these areas. We urge its passage.

At present, U.S. law does not include a definition of transnational repression, which makes it impossible for officials to sufficiently respond. A definition is important to allow officials to understand what transnational repression is and to direct their agencies on reporting, training, and sufficient outreach to and support for victims and potential targets. Codification of a definition for foreign policy purposes in Title 22 should include a detailed description that explains the full scope of transnational repression tactics. Any updates to Title 18, which deals with crimes and criminal activity, should be narrowly tailored to ensure U.S. criminal law can sufficiently address transnational repression without inadvertently criminalizing benign activities or enabling the targeting of individuals simply due to their country of origin. Congressman Schiff has introduced legislation that would update Title 18 with additional authorities related to transnational repression.

Some agencies and bureaus have provided training for officials. But, trainings are not yet routinized or mandated for all officials or employees who may come in contact with perpetrators or victims. Establishing agency-wide trainings for all officials who may encounter the issue will help the U.S. government respond more effectively.

On the sanctions front, the United States possesses a number of targeted sanctions options, including the Global Magnitsky Human Rights Accountability Act; the authorities provided in section 7031(c) of the annual Department of State, Foreign Operations, and Related Programs Appropriations Act; the Khashoggi Ban visa restrictions, and several country-specific sanctions programs. With the exception of the Khashoggi Ban, however, none of these sanctions programs explicitly address transnational repression, and they cover only the most severe cases of transnational repression, such as murder or kidnapping. And while the Khashoggi Ban addresses transnational repression directly, it only imposes visa bans—a weaker measure than the asset freezes included in other sanctions mechanisms. It is also a policy implemented voluntarily by the Biden administration, meaning future administrations would not be legally required to screen visa applicants for activity related to transnational repression.

2) Establish clear pathways for exiled human rights defenders to receive permanent legal status when needed. Democratic governments should consider appropriate mechanisms, including providing special visas, such as humanitarian visas or visas for human rights defenders, activists, and journalists, to help them receive legal status. Countries should also review their asylum processes to ensure that exiled human rights defenders, activists, and journalists are not being denied legal status as a result of illegitimate criminal charges leveled against them by origin country governments. Permanent legal status offers a better safeguard against transnational repression by making the protection of a democracy permanent, reducing a human rights defender's reliance on identification documents from their home country (which can often be cancelled or put them at risk when needing to enter consulates or embassies of their original country for renewal), and potentially allows family reunification, which reduces the risk of coercion by proxy.

3) Urge the executive branch to continue to raise transnational repression as a priority issue with partners and allies. We commend U.S. leadership in the newly launched G7 Rapid Response Mechanism Working Group on Transnational Repression and for signing the Declaration of Principles to Combat Transnational Repression. In addition to these efforts with like-minded governments, the United States must not hesitate to raise this issue directly at the highest levels with perpetrators of transnational repression, even when those perpetrators are close partners such

as Saudi Arabia and India. Transnational repression is a violation of rights and sovereignty and breaks the bond of trust that must exist for deep cooperation between nations. Whether a government engages in transnational repression should be a significant factor determining the nature of bilateral relations and the closeness of any partnership.

> *"Agencies have reported on foreign governments known to engage in [transnational repression] worldwide, some of which receive U.S. arms transfers. However, officials said that a lack of common understanding of TNR hinders efforts to fully track incidents against U.S.-based persons."*

The United States Must Address the Repression of Dissidents

Government Accountability Office

The following viewpoint from the Government Accountability Office proves the growing awareness within the United States about the threat of transnational repression of those living within its borders and calls for more extensive and effective policies by government agencies. According to the Government Accountability Office, this can be achieved best through Congressional action. The organization offers specific recommendations for what Congress can do to help reduce transnational repression. The Government Accountability Office (GAO) is an independent, non-partisan agency that works for the U.S. Congress.

"Agency Actions Needed to Address Harassment of Dissidents and Other Tactics of Transnational Repression in the U.S." by Government Accountability Office (GAO), October 3, 2023. Reproduced with permission.

As you read, consider the following questions:

1. What prompted the GAO to perform this study?
2. What does the GAO claim to be the most effective approach to dealing with this issue?
3. What evidence does the GAO give to prove its assessment that the United States has been lacking in combatting transnational repression?

Transnational repression is when governments use threats or violence to silence dissenters living abroad. The 2018 murder of Jamal Khashoggi—a critic of Saudi Arabia—by Saudi agents in Turkey is a well-known example. But governments also use less visible tactics, like social media threats.

It can be hard to detect the foreign connection to these crimes, and victims may be afraid to report them. And U.S. law doesn't define transnational repression. So federal agencies may not understand how extensive it is in the U.S.

We recommended ways that federal agencies and Congress can enhance their understanding of this repression in the U.S. and abroad.

Highlights

What GAO Found

Foreign governments may use various tactics—from spyware to assault—to silence U.S.-based dissidents. Agencies have worked to track such incidents, generally known as transnational repression (TNR). Agencies have reported on foreign governments known to engage in TNR worldwide, some of which receive U.S. arms transfers. However, officials said that a lack of common understanding of TNR hinders efforts to fully track incidents against U.S.-based persons.

U.S. law does not specifically criminalize TNR, but agencies have used existing tools to penalize individuals for TNR against

U.S.-based persons. State imposed visa restrictions on 76 Saudis believed to have been engaged in acts of TNR, including the murder of U.S. resident Jamal Khashoggi. FBI officials said gaps in U.S. law limit their ability to counter TNR, but DOJ has not developed a DOJ-wide position on the sufficiency of existing laws. Developing such a position may help Congress determine whether new legislation is needed to address TNR.

Section 6 of the Arms Export Control Act (AECA)—which prohibits arms transfers to countries that the President determines are engaged in a consistent pattern of acts of intimidation or harassment against individuals in the U.S.—offers a way to hold some governments accountable for TNR against individuals in the U.S. However, no such determinations have been made, and none of the agencies we spoke with had performed any work related to implementing the statute. Because Section 6 only requires reporting following a positive determination, it is unclear the extent to which the law has ever been considered. Amending its reporting requirement could improve visibility into how, if at all, the law is used.

Why GAO Did This Study

Recent high-profile acts of TNR against U.S.-based persons highlight TNR's threat to national security. Some advocates and members of Congress have called for more accountability for foreign governments that benefit from U.S. arms transfers yet engage in TNR against U.S.-based persons.

GAO was asked to review federal agency efforts to address TNR using available tools, including Section 6 of the AECA. This report examines the extent to which: (1) agencies have collected and analyzed information about the nature and prevalence of TNR against U.S.-based persons; (2) agencies have used available tools to hold individuals accountable for TNR against U.S.-based persons; and (3) the U.S. government has implemented Section 6 of the AECA.

GAO analyzed documents and interviewed officials from nongovernmental organizations and the Departments of State, Defense, Justice, and Homeland Security.

Recommendations

Congress should consider amending the reporting requirement in Section 6 of the AECA to improve visibility into agency or administration decision-making regarding the implementation of the statute. GAO is also making four recommendations, including that DOJ take additional steps to enhance the common understanding of TNR and develop a department-wide position on any gaps in legislation for addressing TNR. DOJ agreed to take additional steps to enhance common understanding of TNR and said it will consider analyzing potential gaps in legislation for addressing TNR.

Matter for Congressional Consideration		
Matter	**Status**	**Comments**
If Congress wants additional visibility into considerations of determinations pursuant to Section 6 of the Arms Export Control Act, which prohibits arms transfers to any country determined to be engaged in a consistent pattern of acts of intimidation or harassment against individuals in the U.S., Congress should consider amending the reporting requirement in Section 6 to include any instances where, for example, the President (a) considered, but ultimately declined, a determination, or (b) delegated the determination to an agency. (Matter for Consideration 1)	Open	While the 118th Congress has introduced several pieces of legislation related to transnational repression, as of March 2024, Congress has not yet considered legislation to modify the reporting requirements related to Section 6 of the Arms Export Control Act.

Recommendations for Executive Action	
Department of Justice	
Recommendation	Status
The Attorney General should ensure that the Assistant Attorney General of the National Security Division and the Director of the Federal Bureau of Investigation, in consultation with the Secretaries of Homeland Security and State, take additional steps to enhance understanding of transnational repression among federal agencies and state and local law enforcement agencies, such as by establishing a formal interagency definition of transnational repression or conducting additional training. (Recommendation 1)	Open In its written comments on the report, DOJ concurred with this recommendation and said that it is already taking such steps through various training exercises and outreach. GAO will continue to monitor DOJ's actions in response to this recommendation.

Department of Justice	
Recommendation	Status
The Attorney General should develop and draft a coordinated, department-wide position on any identified gaps in current legislation for addressing transnational repression and, if appropriate, submit a legislative proposal to the Office of Management and Budget in accordance with OMB Circular A-19. (Recommendation 2)	Open In its written comments on the report, DOJ said that it would be pleased to consider analyzing potential gaps and developing a coordinated, department-wide position, if appropriate. DOJ noted that it is obligated to abide by the established process for the Executive Branch, including OMB Circular A-19, for the development of legislative proposals and for the clearance of Department and Administration views on such proposals. DOJ further noted that it welcomes requests from Congress for technical assistance on legislative proposals by Congress. GAO will continue to monitor DOJ's actions in response to this recommendation.

Department of State	
Recommendation	**Status**
The Secretary of State should ensure that the Assistant Secretaries for Political-Military Affairs and Democracy, Human Rights, and Labor include steps to coordinate with and collect information on transnational repression from other agencies, such as the Departments of Justice and Homeland Security, in its new transnational repression-related tools and guidance to align the arms transfer decisions-making process with the 2023 Conventional Arms Transfer Policy. (Recommendation 3)	Open In its written comments on the report, State concurred with this recommendation and said it will take steps to implement it. GAO will continue to monitor State's actions in response to this recommendation.

Department of State	
Recommendation	**Status**
The Secretary of State should ensure that the Assistant Secretaries for Political-Military Affairs and Democracy, Human Rights, and Labor include steps to coordinate with and collect information on TNR from other agencies, such as the Departments of Justice and Homeland Security, in its new procedures specific to Section 6 of the Arms Export Control Act. (Recommendation 4)	Open In its written comments on the report, State concurred with this recommendation and said it will take steps to implement it. GAO will continue to monitor State's actions in response to this recommendation.

Viewpoint 3

> *"Allowing this activity to continue unchallenged not only abandons and threatens victims of human rights abuses, but also poses a direct threat to the national security of the United States."*

How the U.S. Treasury Is Targeting Repression and Threats to Democracy

U.S. Department of the Treasury

The U.S. Department of the Treasury examines cases of transnational repression from around the world to cite examples of it. It explains how this is happening, which countries it considers "bad actors," and what it is doing to alleviate the problem. The Treasury emphasizes that it is doing more than pointing fingers of blame by taking action to call the offending nations into account. The Department of the Treasury does this in part by imposing sanctions blocking people who engage in transnational repression, which generally involves freezing or seizing their assets. The U.S. Department of the Treasury is the national finance and treasury department of the U.S. federal government.

"Treasury Targets Repression and the Undermining of Democracy" by U.S. Department of the Treasury, December 7, 2021.

As you read, consider the following questions:

1. Based on this viewpoint, has the U.S. Treasury done more than place blame on international governments practicing repression?
2. What can the Treasury Department do to play a role in solving this problem that differs from other areas of the American government?
3. What is the Global Magnitsky Human Rights Accountability Act?

Today, the U.S. Department of the Treasury's Office of Foreign Assets Control (OFAC) is designating 15 actors across three countries in connection with serious human rights abuse and repressive acts targeting innocent civilians, political opponents, and peaceful protestors. As part of a whole-of-government commitment to democracy, Treasury is taking a number of actions aimed at promoting accountability for those who undermine trust in democratic institutions. Treasury is equipped with powerful tools to target the financial systems and flows that allow bad actors to profit from corruption and abuse. In addition, OFAC is designating two entities and two individuals that the Department of State has identified as responsible for certain gross violations of human rights in Iran.

"Ahead of this week's Summit for Democracy, Treasury is targeting over a dozen government officials across three countries in connection with serious human rights abuse that undermines democracy," said Director of the Office of Foreign Assets Control Andrea M. Gacki. "Treasury will continue to defend against authoritarianism, promoting accountability for violent repression of people seeking to exercise their human rights and fundamental freedoms."

Today's actions are taken pursuant to the following authorities: Executive Order (E.O.) 13818, which builds upon and implements the Global Magnitsky Human Rights Accountability Act, and targets perpetrators of corruption and serious human rights abuse; E.O. 13553, which imposes sanctions on certain persons with respect to serious human rights abuses by the Government of Iran; Section 106 of the Countering America's Adversaries Through Sanctions Act (CAATSA), which allows Treasury to designate persons listed by the Secretary of State as responsible for gross violations of human rights against individuals in Iran who seek to expose illegal activity carried out by officials of the Government of Iran, or to obtain, exercise, defend, or promote internationally recognized human rights and freedoms; as well as E.O. 13572, which, among other things, imposes sanctions on certain persons responsible for or complicit in human rights abuses in Syria, as well as senior officials of, or entities owned or controlled by, persons blocked pursuant to E.O. 13572.

Repression and the Undermining of Democracy

Democratic values and human rights are under threat around the world. Human rights defenders, members of civil society groups, journalists, and ordinary people seeking to exercise their right to freedom of expression and right of peaceful assembly face threats of violent repression from authoritarian leaders. Allowing this activity to continue unchallenged not only abandons and threatens victims of human rights abuses, but also poses a direct threat to the national security of the United States. Countries with repressive political regimes are often unstable over the long run, and they export instability regionally and worldwide. These regimes are often a threat to the peace and security of other nations. Standing up for human rights is not only consistent with American values but also U.S. national interests.

Repression in Uganda: Abel Kandiho

As commander of the Ugandan Chieftaincy of Military Intelligence (CMI), Major General Abel Kandiho (Kandiho) and other CMI officers have arrested, detained, and physically abused persons in Uganda. The CMI targeted individuals due to their nationality, political views, or critique of the Ugandan government. Individuals were taken into custody and held, often without legal proceedings, at CMI detention facilities where they were subjected to horrific beatings and other egregious acts by CMI officials, including sexual abuse and electrocutions, often resulting in significant long-term injury and even death. During these incarcerations, victims were kept in solitary confinement and unable to contact friends, family, or legal support. In some cases, Kandiho was personally involved, leading interrogations of detained individuals.

Kandiho is designated pursuant to E.O. 13818 for being a foreign person who is or has been a leader or official of an entity that has engaged in, or whose members have engaged in, serious human rights abuse relating to his tenure.

Repression in Iran: Violent Suppression of Peaceful Protesters and Prisoners of Conscience

The Special Units of Iran's Law Enforcement Forces (LEF Special Units) are the dedicated crowd control and protest suppression unit of Iran's LEF, one of the Government of Iran's main security apparatuses that played a key role in the crackdown on protesters in the aftermath of the disputed Iranian presidential election in 2009. Serious human rights abuses against prisoners detained in the post-election protests also occurred at a detention facility run by the LEF. Treasury designated the LEF pursuant to E.O. 13553 on June 9, 2011, for its role in the post-election crackdown. The LEF Special Units were also involved in the post-election protest suppression in 2009 and have been called upon to forcefully put down multiple nationwide protests since then, including the November 2019 protests resulting from gasoline price increases, during which Iranian security forces killed hundreds of Iranian protestors. The LEF Special Units were one of the main security forces on the ground in November 2019, alongside units of Iran's Islamic Revolutionary Guard Corps (IRGC) and Iran's Basij Resistance Force (Basij), a paramilitary force subordinate to the IRGC. In multiple locations throughout Iran, LEF Special

Units forces, along with those of a subunit, Iran's Counter-Terror Special Forces (NOPO), used excessive and lethal force, firing upon unarmed protestors, including women and children, with automatic weapons. NOPO forces blocked main streets with armed vehicles and fired randomly at crowds with heavy machine guns.

The LEF Special Units and NOPO are being designated pursuant to E.O. 13553 for being persons acting on behalf of the Government of Iran responsible for or complicit in, or responsible for ordering, controlling, or otherwise directing, the commission of serious human rights abuses against persons in Iran or Iranian citizens or residents, or the family members of the foregoing, on or after June 12, 2009, regardless of whether such abuses occurred in Iran. The LEF Special Units are also being designated pursuant to E.O. 13553 for being owned or controlled by or having acted or purported to act for or on behalf of, directly or indirectly, Iran's Law Enforcement Forces. NOPO is also being designated pursuant to E.O. 13553 for being owned or controlled by or having acted or purported to act for or on behalf of, directly or indirectly, the LEF Special Units.

Hassan Karami (Karami) is the commander of the LEF Special Units and has overseen the unit during periods of nationwide unrest during which the LEF Special Units have employed excessive and lethal force against Iranian unarmed protestors, including during November 2019. He was sanctioned by the European Union in April 2021 for his role in the violent response to the November 2019 protests. Mohsen Ebrahimi (Ebrahimi) was appointed commander of NOPO in 2016 and has similarly overseen the unit during several subsequent periods of nationwide unrest during which NOPO employed excessive and lethal force against Iranian unarmed protestors. Seyed Reza Mousavi Azami (Azami) commands a brigade of the LEF Special Units.

Karami and Azami are being designated pursuant to E.O. 13553 for having acted or purported to act for or on behalf of, directly or indirectly, the LEF Special Units. Ebrahimi is being designated pursuant to E.O. 13553 for having acted or purported to act for or on behalf of, directly or indirectly, NOPO.

Gholamreza Soleimani (Soleimani) commands the Basij, one of Iran's most important domestic security resources. The Basij has been heavily involved in violent crackdowns in Iran, including following the June 2009 contested presidential election, and in November 2019, during Soleimani's tenure, when the Basij reportedly were among the Iranian security organizations that collectively killed hundreds of Iranian men, women, and children. Treasury designated the Basij pursuant to E.O. 13553 on June 9, 2011, for, among other activity, its role in the 2009 post-election crackdown. Soleimani was sanctioned by the European Union in April 2021 for his role in the violent response to the November 2019 protests.

Soleimani is being designated pursuant to E.O. 13553 for having acted or purported to act for or on behalf of, directly or indirectly, the Basij.

Leila Vaseghi (Vaseghi), the governor of Qods city, was responsible for issuing an order to the police and other armed forces during the November 2019 protests to shoot unarmed protestors, causing dozens of deaths or injuries. Vaseghi was also sanctioned by the EU in April 2021 for her role in the violent response to the November 2019 protests.

Vaseghi is being designated pursuant to E.O. 13553 for being a person acting on behalf of the Government of Iran (including members of paramilitary organizations) who is responsible for or complicit in, or responsible for ordering, controlling, or otherwise directing, the commission of serious human rights abuses against persons in Iran or Iranian citizens or residents, or the family members of the foregoing, on or after June 12, 2009, regardless of whether such abuses occurred in Iran.

IRGC interrogators Ali Hemmatian (Hemmatian) and Masoud Safdari (Safdari) have long records of physical abuse against Iranian political prisoners at IRGC detention facilities, including at Iran's Evin Prison. Hemmatian employed physical beatings and whippings during interrogation of prisoners, resulting in lasting damage, including cracked bones. He has physically beaten many student activists and women and has also directed, and authored the text of, televised confessions. Safdari has similarly been involved in detainee abuse, to include physical beatings and threatening the families of detainees. He has also managed the recording of televised confessions.

Hemmatian and Safdari are being designated pursuant to E.O. 13553 for being persons acting on behalf of the Government of Iran (including members of paramilitary organizations) responsible for or complicit in, or responsible for ordering, controlling, or otherwise directing, the commission of serious human rights abuses against persons in Iran or Iranian citizens or residents, or the family members of the foregoing, on or after June 12, 2009, regardless of whether such abuses occurred in Iran. On March 9, 2021 the Department of State designated Hemmatian and Safdari pursuant to Section 7031(c) of the Department of State, Foreign Operations, and Related Programs Appropriations Act, 2021, for their involvement in gross violations of human rights.

Zahedan Prison, located in the Sistan and Baluchistan province in southeast Iran, reportedly holds several political prisoners who belong to the Baluch ethnic minority group. According to public reports, on January 3, 2021, Baluch prisoner Hassan Dehvari was executed in Zahedan Prison. Dehvari was sentenced to death for "armed rebellion against the Islamic Rule." His sentence was escalated to execution after he engaged in several acts of peaceful protests, such as signing statements condemning executions of Sunni prisoners and condemning the mistreatment of fellow prisoners in Zahedan Prison. Dehvari addressed an open letter to UN experts protesting his death sentence and requesting help. According to Dehvari's lawyer, his execution was carried out despite a request for retrial pending with the Supreme Court. Dehvari's execution was likely in retaliation for seeking to exercise his right to freedom of expression. According to human rights groups, IRGC officers arrested another Baluch prisoner, Hamid

Reza Koukhan, on August 27, 2020, for reportedly "writing slogans, disrupting national security, and insulting the leadership of Qassem Soleimani" during a protest and sent him to Zahedan Prison in October 2020. Zahedan Prison is responsible for the flagrant denial of the right to liberty of Koukhan for seeking to exercise his right to freedom of expression and his right of peaceful assembly.

Isfahan Central Prison, also known as "Dastgerd Prison," located in Isfahan city, is where, according to media reports, Mostafa Salehi, an electrical generator repairman, was executed on August 5, 2020, after taking part in streets protests in December 2017 and January 2018. According to Human Rights Watch, the prosecutor in Salehi's case accused him of having contacts with foreign intelligence and having "organized the riots." Salehi was convicted of murder for the killing of an IRGC officer during these protests but maintained his innocence and independent media reports suggest that the prosecution authorities failed to provide evidence of his guilt. Isfahan Central Prison is responsible for the flagrant denial of the right to life and liberty of Salehi for seeking to exercise his right to freedom of expression and his right of peaceful assembly.

Zahedan Prison and Isfahan Central Prison are being listed by the Department of State and designated by OFAC pursuant to Section 106 of CAATSA.

Soghra Khodadadi, the current director of Qarchak Women's Prison, was responsible for ordering and directly participating in a violent attack on December 13, 2020, against prisoners of conscience in Ward 8 along with at least 20 other guards. According to publicly available reports, prison guards beat these female prisoners of conscience with batons and stun guns. Khodadadi ordered this attack in retaliation for the prisoners exercising their right to freedom of expression.

Khodadadi is being listed by the Department of State and designated by OFAC pursuant to Section 106 of CAATSA. Qarchak Prison was publicly identified as responsible for certain gross violations of human rights under CAATSA in 2019 and designated in 2020.

Mohammad Karami is a Brigadier General and commands the IRGC South-East Quds Operational Base in Zahedan in Sistan and Baluchistan Province. The Quds Base is officially tasked with ensuring security in Sistan-Baluchistan, including the Saravan border, between Sistan and Baluchistan and Pakistan. According to public reporting, Karami is responsible for the actions of IRGC officers stationed at the Shamsar Base, who according to Amnesty International on February 22, 2021, fired live ammunition at unarmed fuel porters who were seeking to exercise their freedom of expression.

Karami is being listed by the Department of State and designated by OFAC pursuant to Section 106 of CAATSA.

Repression in Syria: Designations of Persons Involved in Deadly Chemical Weapons Attacks Against Civilians, and Designations of Senior Officials of Syrian Intelligence and Security Entities

OFAC is also designating two senior Syrian Air Force officers responsible for chemical weapons attacks on civilians and three senior officers in Syria's repressive security and intelligence apparatus. These senior officials and the organizations they are associated with have imprisoned hundreds of thousands of Syrians who peacefully called for change. Moreover, at least 14,000 prisoners in Syria have allegedly died as a result of torture. Today's designations are another critical step in promoting accountability for the Assad regime's abuses against Syrians.

Tawfiq Muhammad Khadour (Khadour) is a Major General in the Syrian Air Force (SAF), currently in command of the 22nd Air Division. On February 25, 2018, while Khadour commanded the 30th Brigade of the SAF at Dumayr Airbase, airstrikes from the airbase against Eastern Ghouta dropped chemical barrel bombs throughout the area, killing civilians. On April 7, 2018, an attack on Eastern Ghouta launched from Dumayr Airbase, still under

How U.S. Government Agencies Work Together to Combat Repression

Consistent with the goals of this week's Summit for Democracy, the United States is committed to using its full range of tools to counter serious human rights abuse and repressive acts across the world. That is why today we designated multiple actors across three countries in connection with serious human rights abuse and repressive acts targeting political opponents, peaceful protestors, and other individuals pursuant to Executive Orders (E.O.) 13818, 13553, and 13572. The United States also submitted a report, pursuant to section 106 of the Countering America's Adversaries Through Sanctions Act of 2017 (CAATSA), identifying persons who are responsible for certain gross violations of human rights in Iran.

The Department of the Treasury, in consultation with the State Department, targeted military actors in connection with serious human rights abuse. These actors include the commander of the Ugandan Chieftaincy of Military Intelligence, two Syrian Air Force officers responsible for chemical weapons attacks on civilians, and three Syrian intelligence officers in Syria's repressive security and intelligence apparatus. These designations, which include individuals previously sanctioned by the European Union, also bring the United States into closer alignment with allies and partners, reflecting our shared commitment to promoting democracy and respect for human rights.

Additionally, Treasury sanctioned seven Iranian individuals and two Iranian law enforcement entities in connection with serious human rights abuse pursuant to E.O. 13553. Further, pursuant to Section 106 of CAATSA, the Department of State identified two entities and two individuals who are responsible for certain gross violations of internationally recognized human rights in Iran. This action under CAATSA included two prisons, the Zahedan Prison and Isfahan Central Prison, which are responsible for extrajudicial killings and arbitrary detention.

The United States is committed to promoting democracy and accountability for those who abuse human rights around the world. The United States will utilize its full range of tools to highlight and disrupt these abuses of human rights. We will continue to stand in solidarity with the people of these countries and others where abuses and violations of human rights continue to occur.

"Targeting Repression and Supporting Democracy" by Antony J. Blinken. U.S. Department of State, December 7, 2021.

the command of Khadour, included at least two chlorine barrel bombs and a guided missile attack on a humanitarian facility, rendering it inoperable and killing dozens of civilians.

Khadour is being designated under E.O. 13572 for being responsible for or complicit in, or responsible for ordering, controlling, or otherwise directing, or having participated in, the commission of human rights abuses in Syria, including those related to repression.

Muhammad Youssef Al-Hasouri (Al-Hasouri) is a Major General in the SAF in command of the 70th Brigade at T-4 Military Airbase. Al-Hasouri previously served as the deputy commander of the 50th Brigade of the Syrian Air Force at al-Shayrat Airbase. Al-Hasouri personally carried out numerous airstrikes killing Syrian civilians, including chemical weapons attacks. This includes the notorious April 4, 2017, sarin attack at Khan Shaykhun, which killed at least 87 people and for which the European Union sanctioned him.

Al-Hasouri is being designated pursuant to E.O. 13572 for being responsible for or complicit in, or responsible for ordering, controlling, or otherwise directing, or having participated in, the commission of human rights abuses in Syria, including those related to repression.

Adeeb Namer Salameh (Salameh) is the Assistant Director of Syrian Air Force Intelligence (SAFI), an integral component of the Assad regime's repressive security apparatus. Treasury previously designated SAFI on May 18, 2011, for its role in the Assad regime's violent response to civil society protests, including the use of live ammunition against protesters by SAFI forces. Salameh was previously head of SAFI's Aleppo Branch, wherein he was described as one of the most extreme officers and prominent symbols of the Syrian regime's crimes. Salameh was the first to transform a "Shabiha," a term for local criminal gangs, into an irregular militia force under regime control. The militia that Salameh commanded was reportedly responsible for torture, killings, and kidnapping for ransom in the countryside surrounding Salamiyeh, Syria. Salameh gained the nickname "Aleppo's president" after imposing his influence on all the security branches, authorities, and merchants of Aleppo. Salameh has been implicated in major corruption cases for having received large sums of money in exchange for protecting factories and appointing himself as a partner to major investors in Aleppo.

Salameh is being designated for being a senior official of SAFI, an entity whose property and interests in property are blocked pursuant to E.O. 13572.

Qahtan Khalil (Khalil) is a senior SAFI official and is the head of the Security Committee in the South of Syria. He is one of the SAFI officers accused of direct responsibility for the notorious Daraya massacre, which left hundreds dead in the suburbs of Damascus in 2012.

Khalil is being designated for being a senior official of SAFI, an entity whose property and interests in property are blocked pursuant to E.O. 13572.

Kamal al-Hassan (al-Hassan) is the commander of SMI Branch 227 and previously commanded SMI Branch 235, the SMI branch responsible for joint operations with Hizballah. Branch 227 was one of the SMI branches specifically highlighted in images provided by Caesar, a Syrian regime defector—in whose name the Caesar Act was passed into law—who worked as an official forensic photographer for the Syrian military and who courageously revealed thousands of images of detainees who were reportedly tortured and killed.

Al-Hassan is being designated for being a senior official of SMI, an entity whose property and interests in property are blocked pursuant to E.O. 13572.

Sanctions Implications

As a result of today's action, all property and interests in property of the persons designated above that are in the United States or in the possession or control of U.S. persons are blocked and must be reported to OFAC. In addition, any entities that are owned, directly or indirectly, 50 percent or more, by one or more blocked persons are also blocked. Unless authorized by a general or specific license issued by OFAC, or otherwise exempt, all transactions by U.S. persons or within (or transiting) the United States that involve any property or interests in property of designated or otherwise blocked persons are prohibited. The prohibitions include the making of any contribution or provision of funds, goods, or services by, to, or for the benefit of any blocked person or the receipt of any contribution or provision of funds, goods, or services from any such person.

Global Magnitsky

Building upon the Global Magnitsky Human Rights Accountability Act, E.O. 13818 was issued on December 20, 2017, in recognition that the prevalence of human rights abuse and corruption that have their source, in whole or in substantial part, outside the United States, had reached such scope and gravity as to threaten the stability of international political and economic systems. Human rights abuse and corruption undermine the values that form an essential foundation of stable, secure, and functioning societies; have devastating impacts on individuals; weaken democratic institutions; degrade the rule of law; perpetuate violent conflicts; facilitate the activities of dangerous persons; and undermine economic markets. The United States seeks to impose tangible and significant consequences on those who commit serious human rights abuse or engage in corruption, as well as to protect the financial system of the United States from abuse by these same persons.

Viewpoint 4

> *"The ideological rift between platforms like TikTok and western democratic values therefore extends beyond mere business challenges. It underscores a profound conflict of values."*

China Uses Technology to Support Transnational Repression

Ge Chen

In this viewpoint Ge Chen explains how China uses the social media app TikTok—which has become a global sensation—to censor dissident voices around the world. It is essentially necessary for the platform's parent company to work with the Chinese government on this due to strict censorship laws in China, as it would risk being banned otherwise. However, since the app is used in various Western democracies, including the United States, it brings into question whether allowing the use of TikTok in the U.S. is supporting China's censorship and repression. Censorship on social media is just one aspect of China's campaign of transnational repression, and although it may have undesirable economic impacts for the U.S. to ban TikTok, it would also show its commitment to democratic values. Ge Chen is an assistant professor in global media and information law at Durham University in the United Kingdom.

"Digital Platforms Like TikTok Help China Extend Its Censorship Regime Across Borders," by Ge Chen, The Conversation, December 11, 2023, https://theconversation.com/digital-platforms-like-tiktok-could-help-china-extend-its-censorship-regime-across-borders-204322. Licensed under CC BY-ND 4.0 International.

As you read, consider the following questions:

1. What does it mean to "live silently"?
2. According to this viewpoint, how does China engage in economic coercion?
3. According to the author, what is China's core objective?

China's drive to expand its influence through soft power mechanisms like censorship is coming into sharper focus, especially under Xi Jinping's leadership. Recently, the social media app TikTok has become a prominent symbol of this global strategy.

The platform consistently denies that its Chinese parent company, ByteDance, is close to China's government. "ByteDance is not owned or controlled by the Chinese government. It is a private company," TikTok's CEO Shou Zi Chew said. However, U.S. congressional hearings and discussions about potential bans this year may suggest that there are suspicions in some quarters of other countries suspect a deeper, more intricate connection.

The crux of the matter lies in understanding how TikTok, and platforms like it, fit into China's wider interests in spreading its culture, enhancing its global influence and censoring views it objects to across national borders.

At first glance, TikTok provides light-hearted entertainment via catchy dances and comedic sketches. Yet, its content strategy largely reflects a prevalent ethos in China—to "live silently".

This essentially means navigating the digital space in a seemingly non-confrontational manner, being less critical, or at least overtly so, of the Chinese government.

Given the myriad of censorship laws in China, this approach may be both strategic and necessary for TikTok. It reportedly ensures that content creators steer clear of potential controversies. By aligning itself with the Chinese government's narrative, TikTok would certainly reduce its chances of being banned in China.

Such an ethos, however, starkly contrasts with those of western democracies that champion freedom of expression, even when it encompasses controversial or unpopular opinions.

The U.S. Supreme Court, for instance, adheres to a constitutional doctrine which holds that the American government cannot prohibit "expression of an idea simply because society finds the idea itself offensive or disagreeable".

These two divergent philosophies are at the heart of the debate in western countries over TikTok and a broader narrative about how digital platforms can become tools of the state.

When Censorship Meets Capitalism

The potential and temptation for China to exert censorship across borders gets magnified when it's intertwined with global economic interests. China's emphasis on cyber sovereignty and efforts to mold digital standards globally along with its aspirations to position itself at the helm of the digital era are closely aligned with its wider geopolitical goals.

Projects such as the Belt and Road Initiative further underscore China's ambitions, where "soft power" and censorship combine to become a formidable tool of influence.

Such global ambitions are intricately tied to China's economic prowess. Using the promise of access to its vast market and investments, China has been criticised for exerting what has been described as "economic coercion." Governments and corporations, eager for a slice of the pie, might find themselves compromising their principles, including freedom of expression.

This economic leverage becomes a subtle yet powerful tool, potentially making nations or businesses think twice about opposing or criticizing China's policies.

Today, global tech giants find themselves having to balance profits against democratic principles if they want to tap into China's vast and lucrative markets. The conundrum isn't just about TikTok's content policies. It's a reflection of the broader challenges global corporations face, balancing profit motives with foundational principles.

A Digital Divide

China's efforts to exert influence go beyond mere content curation. Its economic prowess allows it to deploy what some academics have called "transnational repression"—a potent tool in the party-state's transnational censorship arsenal.

There's evidence that China has used a combination of digital platforms, surveillance technology, and international collaborations to suppress dissent. This is not just happening domestically, but also among its diaspora.

If governments and corporations compromise their foundational values to access China's markets and resources, it extends the regime's control, ensuring that criticism and challenges to its authority are curtailed globally.

The ideological rift between platforms like TikTok and western democratic values therefore extends beyond mere business challenges. It underscores a profound conflict of values. Digital platforms hailing from China, such as TikTok, operate within a framework that mandates content curation in line with the Chinese government's directives.

Amplified Influence

China's unwavering adherence to its ideological principles, including campaigns such as "class struggle", can be traced back to historical movements in China like the "Yan'an Rectification Movement" of 1942. The strategies may have changed, but the core objective remains unaltered: to amplify the influence of an assertive, authoritarian regime.

In today's interconnected world, digital platforms are not just sources of entertainment. Instead, they represent the convergence of technology, politics and culture. TikTok, and its global reach, is a testament to this fusion. With its catchy challenges and trending dances, it is not just an entertainment app, but a digital stage where business, entertainment and geopolitics converge.

As we continue to interact with these platforms, it's vital to understand these underlying currents, recognising the geopolitical games at play beneath the surface of viral trends and social media challenges.

Periodical and Internet Sources Bibliography

The following articles have been selected to supplement the diverse views presented in this chapter.

Mo Abbas, "The Chinese Government Tried to Silence Them. It Backfired," NBC News, March 3, 2024. https://www.nbcnews.com/news/world/china-dissidents-abroad-transnational-repression-rcna140146

Sir Christopher Chope, "Transnational Repression as a Growing Threat to the Rule of Law and Human Rights," Parliamentary Assembly. https://rm.coe.int/transnational-repression-as-a-growing-threat-to-the-rule-of-law-and-hu/1680ab5b07

Alexander Dukalskis, Saipira Furstenberg, and Redmond Scales, "The Long Arm and the Iron Fist: Authoritarian Crackdowns and Transnational Repression," *Journal of Conflict Resolution*, July 13, 2023. https://journals.sagepub.com/doi/10.1177/00220027231188896

Jason P. Hipp, Emily Merrifield, and Susanna D. Evarts, "Transnational Repression Increasingly Reaches Into the United States," Just Security, April 4, 2023. https://www.justsecurity.org/85785/transnational-repression-increasingly-reaches-into-the-united-states/

Joshua Kurlantzick and Abigail McGowan, "The Specter of Transnational Repression," Council on Foreign Relations, December 27, 2023. https://www.cfr.org/blog/specter-transnational-repression

Yasmeen Serhan, "How Authoritarian Regimes are Stepping Up Repression Far Beyond Their Borders," *Time*, October 2, 2023. https://time.com/6319450/transnational-repression-nijjar-khashoggi/

Lily Sparks, "Repression is Being Exposed," Human Rights Watch, March 28, 2024. https://www.hrw.org/news/2024/03/28/repression-being-exported

Gerasimos Tsourapas, "Global Autocracies: Strategies of Transnational Repression, Legitimation, and Co-Optation in World Politics," *International Studies Review*, August 29, 2020. https://academic.oup.com/isr/article/23/3/616/5899220

Chapter 2

Should Western Democracies Help Prevent Repression in Other Countries?

Chapter Preface

Chapter 2 delves deeper into the definition of transnational repression and considers whether the U.S. has done enough to help prevent and stop transnational repression. It also examines some of the cases in which the U.S.'s attempts to prevent "repression" by Communists crossed the line and became repressive itself.

One viewpoint provides a history lesson on the Cold War (1947–1991), during which time the U.S. engaged in wars in Korea and Vietnam and became involved in military campaigns in many other countries where there was a perceived threat of Communist influence. Others explore the moral obligations of every nation to accept basic freedoms and human rights of all its citizens and those who left to live in other countries. Another emphasizes the need for the international community to stop transnational repression.

After all, it is argued, how can anyone be blamed for fleeing repressive countries that do not allow them to express their feelings and viewpoints? And how can anyone accept the repression of those governments meted out to those who do escape? Some viewpoints in Chapter 2 delve into the notion of freedom for all and the role of the U.S., the United Nations, international justice systems, and other Western democracies in stopping repression and extrajudicial killings in other countries.

This chapter expresses more historical perspective and ethical arguments about what rights all humans should be granted and the role the international community should play in enforcing this rather than practical solutions, but without a moral compass there would be little opportunity to form a strong opinion or have a debate on this subject. Only through discussion and debate, however, can solutions be offered and carried out.

Viewpoint 1

> *"Much remains to be revealed on the United States' involvement in Chile's military coup, and its subsequent support for Pinochet's bloody dictatorship: the CIA is reluctant to release the complete files on the issue."*

How the U.S. Repressed Chileans to Prevent the Spread of Communism

Edu Montesanti

In this excerpted viewpoint Edu Montesanti explains how the U.S. engaged in a campaign to repress socialists in Chile during the Cold War, which came to a head when Chilean President Salvador Allende was overthrown during a U.S.-backed military coup on September 11, 1973. Even though it was the Chilean military that led the coup, the U.S. provided a great deal of financial and logistical support to make this happen. After the coup, many other Chileans who were believed to be socialists, Marxists, and communists were imprisoned or even killed. Declassified CIA documents discussed in the viewpoint corroborate claims that the United States played an active role in this regime of repression. Edu Montesanti is a Brazilian-Italian journalist, writer, teacher, and translator.

"The Forgotten Chilean 9/11, Incomparably Worse than the American 9/11," by Edu Montesanti, Orinoco Tribune, October 16, 2023, https://orinocotribune.com/the-forgotten-chilean-9-11-incomparably-worse-than-the-american-9-11-chomsky-interview/.

As you read, consider the following questions:

1. How did the U.S. try to exert influence over the 1970 Chilean elections, according to this viewpoint?
2. What happened to people who were believed to be socialists, Marxists, or other political enemies after the coup in Chile?
3. Who was Henry Kissinger? What was his role in the U.S.'s involvement with Chile?

Salvador Allende, a self-proclaimed Marxist and member of the Socialist Party of Chile, had promised in his presidential campaign to nationalize copper companies, mostly owned by Americans, a big business in Chile. Amidst the Cold War, facing the socialist island of Cuba in permanent revolution, against the historic American imperialism and the ills of the capitalist system, Washington was already expressing concern about Allende's rise in the southern hemisphere, much before he took office as president of one of the more advanced countries at education in the region.

In the months leading up to the Chilean elections of September 4, 1970, a Friday, won by Allende, the U.S. spent millions of dollars into the South American country in a "spoiling operation," much of which was propaganda aimed at preventing Allende from taking power and intensifying political polarization among the Chileans.

Chilean general René Schneider opposed that plot: he ended up murdered on October 23, 1970. About that assassination, the CBS News' 60 Minutes show reported, on September 9, 2001:

> In Chile, the assassination of General Schneider remains the historical equivalent of the assassination of John F. Kennedy: a cruel and shocking political crime that shook the nation. In the United States, the murder of Schneider has become one of the most renowned case studies of CIA efforts to "neutralize" a foreign leader who stood in the way of U.S. objectives.

A CIA report from October 23, 1973, declassified in 2000 and published on the National Security Archive (NSA) website, a U.S. non-governmental body, confirms that Schneider's murder was a plot to overthrow Allende. In this document, the CIA also raises the option of assassinating the newly elected president of Chile.

According to a 1975 U.S. Senate report entitled Secret Action in Chile/1963-1973, the U.S. spent $8 million on secret actions between 1970 and the 1973 coup alone. The newspaper *El Mecurio*, Chile's largest and opposed to Allende, received $1.5 million from the CIA.

The U.S. President Richard Nixon (1969-1974) and Henry Kissinger, his national security advisor, saw the new democratically elected president in Chile as a threat to U.S. interests.

The Washington regime tried everything to prevent Allende from taking office. President Nixon acknowledged that he had given instructions to "do anything short of a Dominican-type action" to keep the democratically elected president of Chile from assuming office, according to a White House audio published by the NSA.

All that, in vain: on November 3, 1970, the elected socialist president took power. "Chile voted calmly to have a Marxist-Leninist state, the first nation in the world to make this choice freely and knowingly," dramatically reported U.S. Ambassador to Chile Edward Korry to the US State Department, in a cable titled "Allende Wins" sent on September 4, 1970.

"We have suffered a grievous defeat; the consequences will be domestic and international; the repercussions will have immediate impact in some lands and delayed effect in others," wrote the American diplomat. As Kissinger told Nixon by phone about the Chilean military, for the failed coup: "a pretty incompetent bunch", according to a documented transcript released by the NSA last August.

"The [congressional] election is tomorrow and the [presidential] inauguration is [November] third. What they could

Transnational Repression Is Becoming Normalized

The rise of transnational repression—ranging from digital threats, family intimidation, and spyware to abductions, assassinations, illegal deportations, and Interpol abuse—has demonstrated that activists, diaspora groups, and dissidents cannot be ensured of their safety even outside of their home countries.

According to a new report from Freedom House, authoritarian states have normalized and institutionalized tools of transnational repression to control citizens beyond their own borders, which found that 38 states have used physical transnational repression in 91 host countries since 2014. Freedom House highlighted exiles living in Canada, Germany, South Africa, Sweden, Thailand, Turkey, Ukraine, the United Kingdom, and the United States as facing serious threats of transnational repression. Moreover, some host states are actively facilitating repression efforts by detaining or deporting exiles at the origin countries' request.

Joshua Kurlantzick has chronicled Southeast Asia's widespread transnational repression and government impunity in previous Asia Unbound blogs. For instance, Vietnam allegedly kidnapped a former oil executive seeking asylum in Germany following accusations of corruption in 2017. Freedom House notes that Thailand has long served as a refuge for exiles facing political repression, but the Thai government often cooperates with foreign governments seeking to apprehend their citizens.

The phenomenon drew widespread attention following Saudi Arabia's 2018 killing of the *Washington Post* journalist Jamal Khashoggi at its consulate in Istanbul, Turkey. Recently, the assassination of a Sikh separatist in Canada and the attempted killing of another in the United States linked to Indian government agents confirms that transnational repression is not limited to nondemocratic states. During the war on terror, the United States established an extraordinary rendition and detention program in partnership with more than 50 foreign governments and unilaterally killed Osama Bin Laden, the mastermind of the September 11 attacks, in Pakistan.

To counter this coercive control, Freedom House advocates accountability through targeted sanctions, protecting the right to asylum, and guarding against abuses of Interpol's Red Notice, among many thorough policy recommendations.

"The Specter of Transnational Repression," by Joshua Kurlantzick and Abigail McGowan. Council on Foreign Relations, December 27, 2023.

have done was prevent the Congress from meeting. But that hasn't been done. It's close, but it's probably too late. "The next move should have been a government takeover [by the military], but that hasn't happened," added the powerful U.S. state secretary and presidential advisor.

Peter Kornbluh, director of the Chile Documentation Project at the Washington-based U.S. National Security Archive, and author of the book *The Pinochet File: A Declassified Dossier on Atrocity and Accountability*, notes that in the conversation between Kissinger and Nixon, "They say nothing that alludes to regret over the assassination of General Schneider; they are totally focused on the incompetence of the Chilean military, which failed to execute the coup to seize power, shut down Congress and block Allende's inauguration."

The CIA then began to hold meetings with the Chilean military in order to provoke a coup. A document from October 23, 1973, declassified in 2000 in the U.S., and published by the NSA, proves the plot.

"The station [the CIA in Santiago] has done excellent job of guiding Chileans to point today where a military solution is at least an option for them," is read in the top secret cable reproduced above, which mentions conversations between American officials and Chilean coup plotters for the "military solution" in the South American country.

In this memo entitled *CIA Activities in Chile*, the American Central Intelligence Agency acknowledged direct participation in the Chilean coup, and earlier.

> The CIA's secret operations on Chilean ground date back to the previous decade. It also mentioned the participation of covert agents, and employees of all elements of the Intelligence Community, with respect to the assassination of President Salvador Allende in September 1973. It is believed that he committed suicide.

In another passage, the CIA said that,

> In the 1960s and 1970s, as part of the U.S. government's policy of trying to influence events in Chile, the CIA undertook specific secret projects in Chile. (...) The main objective—strongly rooted in the politics of the time—was to discredit political leaders with Marxist tendencies, especially Dr. Salvador Allende, and to strengthen and encourage their civilian and military opponents in order to prevent them from taking power.

The following excerpt states, too, that "the CIA actively supported the Military Junta after Allende's overthrow," and "many Pinochet officials were involved in systematic and widespread human rights abuses after Allende's overthrow. Some of them were close to or agents of CIA, or US military."

[...]

The governmental *Archivo Nacional de Chile* records that, "From September 11, 1973, the civil-military dictatorship began to strictly apply the National Security Doctrine, classifying Chileans as internal enemies, dangerous subjects, Marxists, or terrorists just for thinking differently. The exile and uprooting of thousands of compatriots was another tool of the regime to systematically violate human rights, and impose its 'Cleansing Operation' across the country."

The Memoria Chilena website, from the National Library of Chile, recalls the sea of blood that became Santiago's National Stadium, from the first moments after Allende's overthrow:

> Thousands of men were confined to the National Stadium, while their wives and families gathered outside to find out what conditions they were in. Inside, the detainees were subjected to electrical torture and beatings, psychological harassment, poor nutrition, and overcrowding situations that led to the death of several dozen of them [in a very short period of time]. The places of detention were changing rooms, living rooms, and bathrooms. The periods of confinement in the facilities varied: some were released after a few weeks, others were transferred to concentration camps.

Under the title *Henry Kissinger's Documented Legacy*, the NSA published in May 2023 a series of documents about the activities of the then-American Secretary of State during the first years of the military dictatorship in Chile, including Kissinger's private meeting with Pinochet, which until then was kept under a state secret.

"A Declassified Dossier on HAK's Controversial Historical Legacy, on His 100th Birthday Archive Posts Revealing Records of Kissinger's Role in Secret Bombing Campaigns in Cambodia, Illegal Domestic Spying, Support for Dictators and Dirty Wars Abroad" is read in the subtitle of the publications on the U.S. non-governmental website.

Henry Kissinger was Secretary of State during the Republican administrations of Presidents Richard Nixon and Gerald Ford (1974-1977), and served as Nixon's assistant for national security.

In June 1976, when the military coup in Chile was about to reach its third anniversary and the American president was Ford, Kissinger secretly visited Pinochet, congratulating him on his "great service to the West in overthrowing Allende," according to a documented transcript.

At that meeting, the American official, whose advisors in the U.S. had recommended that he press on the Chilean dictator on human rights violations, also told Pinochet: "We want to help, not undermine you. We are sympathetic with what you are trying to do here,"

Much remains to be revealed on the United States' involvement in Chile's military coup, and its subsequent support for Pinochet's bloody dictatorship: the CIA is reluctant to release the complete files on the issue.

The 9/11 in Chile, closely supported by the Washington regime, had unwanted consequences for the Chileans. Contacted by this report to comment on the anniversary of the military coup in Chile, Noam Chomsky regrets that the Chilean 9/11 has been forgotten in the region and ignored throughout the world, as a serious state terrorism sponsored by a foreign government. This is due to what the American intellectual considers a byproduct of American media imposition, “the United States’ backyard” as many in the U.S. consider, or even openly say.

[…]

Viewpoint 2

> *"The two superpowers continually antagonized each other through political maneuvering, military coalitions, espionage, propaganda, arms buildups, economic aid, and proxy wars between other nations."*

The Cold War Was a Turning Point in U.S. Involvement in Other Countries

John F. Kennedy Presidential Library

The Cold War between the communist Soviet Union and capitalist democratic United States lasted about four decades and greatly affected the world economically, politically, and militarily. That period, and the tension that still exists between the two superpowers, continues to affect relations around the globe. It can be rightfully claimed that transnational repression and extrajudicial killings are at least to some extent a reflection of unhealthy relationships between the superpowers due to the force used by both the Soviet Union and the U.S. to control the spread of the opposing ideology. This viewpoint explains how the Cold War planted the seeds for many conflicts that came after it. The John F. Kennedy Presidential Library is dedicated to the memory of former President John F. Kennedy. Its website includes research and materials from the Kennedy administration.

As you read, consider the following questions:

1. What are some ways in which the Kennedy administration tried to prevent the spread of Communism during the Cold War?
2. How did the Cold War demonstrate a change in international policy for the United States?
3. According to this viewpoint, what was the United States' involvement in Vietnam?

After World War II, the United States and its allies, and the Soviet Union and its satellite states began a decades-long struggle for supremacy known as the Cold War. Soldiers of the Soviet Union and the United States did not do battle directly during the Cold War. But the two superpowers continually antagonized each other through political maneuvering, military coalitions, espionage, propaganda, arms buildups, economic aid, and proxy wars between other nations.

From Allies to Adversaries

The Soviet Union and the United States had fought as allies against Nazi Germany during World War II. But the alliance began to crumble as soon as the war in Europe ended in May 1945. Tensions were apparent in July during the Potsdam Conference, where the victorious Allies negotiated the joint occupation of Germany.

The Soviet Union was determined to have a buffer zone between its borders and Western Europe. It set up pro-communist regimes in Poland, Hungary, Bulgaria, Czechoslovakia, Romania, Albania, and eventually in East Germany.

As the Soviets tightened their grip on Eastern Europe, the United States embarked on a policy of containment to prevent the spread of Soviet and communist influence in Western European nations such as France, Italy, and Greece.

During the 1940s, the United States reversed its traditional reluctance to become involved in European affairs. The Truman

Doctrine (1947) pledged aid to governments threatened by communist subversion. The Marshall Plan (1947) provided billions of dollars in economic assistance to eliminate the political instability that could open the way for communist takeovers of democratically elected governments.

France, England, and the United States administered sectors of the city of Berlin, deep inside communist East Germany. When the Soviets cut off all road and rail traffic to the city in 1948, the United States and Great Britain responded with a massive airlift that supplied the besieged city for 231 days until the blockade was lifted. In 1949, the United States joined the North Atlantic Treaty Organization (NATO), the first mutual security and military alliance in American history. The establishment of NATO also spurred the Soviet Union to create an alliance with the communist governments of Eastern Europe that was formalized in 1955 by the Warsaw Pact.

The Worldwide Cold War

In Europe, the dividing line between East and West remained essentially frozen during the next decades. But conflict spread to Asia, Africa, and Latin America. The struggle to overthrow colonial regimes frequently became entangled in Cold War tensions, and the superpowers competed to influence anti-colonial movements.

In 1949, the communists triumphed in the Chinese civil war, and the world's most populous nation joined the Soviet Union as a Cold War adversary. In 1950, North Korea invaded South Korea, and the United Nations and the United States sent troops and military aid. Communist China intervened to support North Korea, and bloody campaigns stretched on for three years until a truce was signed in 1953.

In 1954, the colonial French regime fell in Vietnam.

The United States supported a military government in South Vietnam and worked to prevent free elections that might have unified the country under the control of communist North Vietnam. In response to the threat, the Southeast Asia Treaty

Organization (SEATO) was formed in 1955 to prevent communist expansion, and President Eisenhower sent some 700 military personnel as well as military and economic aid to the government of South Vietnam. The effort was foundering when John F. Kennedy took office.

Closer to home, the Cuban resistance movement led by Fidel Castro deposed the pro-American military dictatorship of Fulgencio Batista in 1959. Castro's Cuba quickly became militarily and economically dependent on the Soviet Union. The United States' main rival in the Cold War had established a foothold just ninety miles off the coast of Florida.

Kennedy and the Cold War

Cold War rhetoric dominated the 1960 presidential campaign. Senator John F. Kennedy and Vice President Richard M. Nixon both pledged to strengthen American military forces and promised a tough stance against the Soviet Union and international communism. Kennedy warned of the Soviet's growing arsenal of intercontinental ballistic missiles and pledged to revitalize American nuclear forces. He also criticized the Eisenhower administration for permitting the establishment of a pro-Soviet government in Cuba.

John F. Kennedy was the first American president born in the 20th century. The Cold War and the nuclear arms race with the Soviet Union were vital international issues throughout his political career. His inaugural address stressed the contest between the free world and the communist world, and he pledged that the American people would "pay any price, bear any burden, meet any hardship, support any friend, oppose any foe to assure the survival and success of liberty."

The Bay of Pigs

Before his inauguration, JFK was briefed on a plan drafted during the Eisenhower administration to train Cuban exiles for an invasion of their homeland. The plan anticipated that support from the Cuban people and perhaps even elements of the Cuban military would lead to the overthrow of Castro and the establishment of a non-communist government friendly to the United States.

Kennedy approved the operation and some 1,400 exiles landed at Cuba's Bay of Pigs on April 17. The entire force was either killed or captured, and Kennedy took full responsibility for the failure of the operation.

The Arms Race

In June 1961, Kennedy met with Soviet leader Nikita Khrushchev in Vienna, Austria. Kennedy was surprised by Khrushchev's combative tone during the summit. At one point, Khrushchev threatened to cut off Allied access to Berlin. The Soviet leader pointed out the Lenin Peace Medals he was wearing, and Kennedy answered, "I hope you keep them." Just two months later, Khrushchev ordered the construction of the Berlin Wall to stop the flood of East Germans into West Germany.

As a result of these threatening developments, Kennedy ordered substantial increases in American intercontinental ballistic missile forces. He also added five new army divisions and increased the nation's air power and military reserves. The Soviets meanwhile resumed nuclear testing and President Kennedy responded by reluctantly reactivating American tests in early 1962.

The Cuban Missile Crisis

In the summer of 1962, Khrushchev reached a secret agreement with the Cuban government to supply nuclear missiles capable of protecting the island against another U.S.-sponsored invasion. In mid-October, American spy planes photographed the missile sites under construction. Kennedy responded by placing a naval blockade, which he referred to as a "quarantine," around Cuba. He also demanded the removal of the missiles and the destruction of the sites. Recognizing that the crisis could easily escalate into nuclear war, Khrushchev finally agreed to remove the missiles in return for an American pledge not to reinvade Cuba. But the end of Cuban Missile Crisis did little to ease the tensions of the Cold War. The Soviet leader decided to commit whatever resources were required for upgrading the Soviet nuclear strike force. His decision led to a major escalation of the nuclear arms race.

In June 1963, President Kennedy spoke at the American University commencement in Washington, DC. He urged Americans to critically reexamine Cold War stereotypes and myths and called for a strategy of peace that would make the world safe for diversity. In the final months of the Kennedy presidency Cold War tensions seemed to soften as the Limited Nuclear Test Ban Treaty was negotiated and signed. In addition, Washington and Moscow established a direct line of communication known as the "Hotline" to help reduce the possibility of war by miscalculation.

Vietnam

In May 1961, JFK had authorized sending 500 Special Forces troops and military advisers to assist the government of South Vietnam. They joined 700 Americans already sent by the Eisenhower administration. In February 1962, the president sent an additional 12,000 military advisers to support the South Vietnamese army. By early November 1963, the number of U.S. military advisers had reached 16,000.

Even as the military commitment in Vietnam grew, JFK told an interviewer, "In the final analysis, it is their war. They are the ones who have to win it or lose it. We can help them, we can give them equipment, we can send our men out there as advisers, but they have to win it—the people of Vietnam against the Communists . . . But I don't agree with those who say we should withdraw. That would be a great mistake . . . [The United States] made this effort to defend Europe. Now Europe is quite secure. We also have to participate—we may not like it—in the defense of Asia." In the final weeks of his life, JFK wrestled with the need to decide the future of the United States commitment in Vietnam—and very likely had not made a final decision before his death.

Viewpoint 3

> *"Over the years, the UDHR has been consistently referred to as a steadfast cornerstone of human rights internationally. It has been likened to 'a code of life for our modern world', the '20th-century Magna Carta' and an 'international yardstick with which governments can measure progress in the field of human rights'."*

Human Rights Are Everybody's Business

Kathryn McNeilly

In this viewpoint Kathryn McNeilly discusses the Universal Declaration of Human Rights (UDHR), which was adopted by the United Nations general assembly in 1948 and has served as the basis for discussions around human rights ever since. McNeilly explains that recent events, such as the conflicts in Gaza and Ukraine, have presented new challenges for human rights and has forced the international community to question how they can work to protect civilians from repression and death in these countries. While the UDHR has played an important role in the history of human rights, it is not a legally enforceable document. However, it has caused certain human rights to be viewed as universally applicable, which can urge

"How the Universal Declaration of Human Rights Can Guide Governments Through the Turmoil of 2024," by Kathryn McNeilly, The Conversation, February 2, 2024, https://theconversation.com/how-the-universal-declaration-of-human-rights-can-guide-governments-through-the-turmoil-of-2024-219437.

countries and organizations like the United Nations to intervene when another country is violating them. Kathryn McNeilly is a professor of law in the School of Law at Queen's University Belfast in Northern Ireland.

As you read, consider the following questions:

1. What are some of the human rights in the UDHR mentioned in this viewpoint?
2. Which rights included in the UDHR are violated by transnational repression and extrajudicial killing?
3. What does the UDHR aim to do?

In a landscape of seemingly increasing global crises, the Universal Declaration of Human Rights (UDHR) celebrated its 75th anniversary in December 2023.

With the horrors of the second world war a recent memory, the UDHR was created as a set of international standards offering more protection for people in times of difficulty, and in the hope that "atrocities like those of that conflict [would never] happen again".

However, 75 years on, the world is facing major human rights challenges again. Human rights violations are being regularly reported in conflicts, most recently in Ukraine and Gaza. For instance, in Ukraine, summary executions, torture, sexual violence, and enforced disappearances are among the issues that have been noted by the UN. In Gaza, the UN has commented on unlawful killings of civilians.

Human rights barrister Baroness Helena Kennedy is co-chairing a high level group looking at enforced disappearances of Ukrainian children by Russian occupying forces, a mechanism for them to be returned, as well as a new international legal basis for the protection of children's rights in armed conflict.

Commenting on this work, Baroness Kennedy said: "The requirement to establish a mechanism in line with international human rights standards is clear, as is the necessity for collaboration at [the] international level among legal experts, organizations—including the United Nations—and states, which must better enforce existing UN mechanisms on the protection of children in conflict."

In this context, it is apt to consider more of what the UDHR is, how states have engaged with it across history, and the hurdles that it faces in 2024.

What Is the UDHR?

Adopted by the UN general assembly on December 10, 1948, in a vote of 48 in favour and 8 abstaining, the UDHR outlines a range of human rights that states agreed were to be universally protected.

These include the right to life, the right to be free from slavery, the right to an adequate standard of living, and the right to education, to name a few. While not legally binding, the document aims to provide a "common standard of achievement for all peoples and all nations". It has proved significant in the intervening decades, laying down provisions that have informed the binding international human rights treaties, subsequently enacted by the UN.

Following the UDHR's adoption, in 1950 the general assembly invited all of its then 60 member states and wider interested organisations to mark December 10 annually as Human Rights Day. Celebration of Human Rights Day has taken place ever since across the world.

Research reveals that on these anniversaries the document was used by states to discuss and support legally binding rights such as freedom from torture, the rights of women and children, and protection from discrimination, coinciding with the drafting of new legal documents on these topics.

When wider discussions started to happen around decolonization in the 1950s and 60s, cold war tensions and détente in the 1970s–80s, and the challenges of technological change from the 1990s onwards, the UDHR was used as a reference point to map human rights and discuss where they needed to develop further. This was also the case for global security as well as environmental and financial crises in the 1990s and 2000s.

During these times, the UDHR offered guidance and a vehicle for analysis. One example is the human rights implications of the cold war arms race. The UDHR both signalled towards the need for commitment to peace—as Eleanor Roosevelt, who chaired the drafting committee, commented during its adoption, "the declaration was inspired by a sincere desire for peace"—as well as highlighted where states were placing human rights under threat through nuclear policies.

Over the years, the UDHR has been consistently referred to as a steadfast cornerstone of human rights internationally. It has been likened to "a code of life for our modern world", the "20th-century Magna Carta" and an "international yardstick with which governments can measure progress in the field of human rights".

Nevertheless, continuing effort has been necessary to implement the rights that the UDHR protects. In 1973, the UN secretary-general, Kurt Waldheim, reflected on this, stating: "It is well that we remind ourselves of the realism, as well as the idealism, of those who created that great Declaration … it would be wrong to say that the fundamental freedoms set out in the Declaration have been universally achieved."

The UDHR Today

As in earlier decades in times of emergency, conflict, and global change, states do not always fully implement the rights contained in the UDHR. Examples recently highlighted by the UN include the right to participate in elections, effective administration of justice and law enforcement, and the right to an adequate standard of living, such as access to water and sanitation.

The UDHR's recognition and protection of the "the equal and inalienable rights of all members of the human family", as outlined in its preamble, is still highly relevant, especially because of the contemporary crises facing human rights.

The fundamental protections outlined in this document, adopted in 1948, still have an enduring and guiding role, although significant challenges to these protections remain. They require the ongoing attention of the international community.

Viewpoint 4

> *"People must be able to move freely and choose a place of residence within a country without restrictions, including establishing a purpose or reason for doing so."*

Freedom of Movement Should Be Universal

Australian Human Rights Commission

This viewpoint from the Australian Human Rights Commission offers a factual rundown of international law that plainly states the rights of people to move freely from one country to another without the threat of repression. The viewpoint was written in response to the growing number of dissidents who have been targeted for persecution in recent times. The author of this viewpoint points out that there are limitations to freedom of movement, but that essentially citizens should be able to leave and enter their own countries—and leave any other country—without restriction. The Australian Human Rights Commission is a national human rights institution of Australia that is funded by but operates independently from the Australian Government.

As you read, consider the following questions:

1. What are the limitations to complete freedom for dissidents who have left their countries to live in Australia, according to this viewpoint?

2. How does the right to free movement relate to transnational repression?
3. According to this viewpoint, is preventing a non-citizen from entering the country against international law?

ICCPR Article 12 states:

1. Everyone lawfully within the territory of a State shall, within that territory, have the right to liberty of movement and freedom to choose his residence.
2. Everyone shall be free to leave any country, including his own.
3. The above-mentioned rights shall not be subject to any restrictions except those which are provided by law, are necessary to protect national security, public order (ordre public), public health or morals or the rights and freedoms of others and are consistent with the other rights recognized in the present Covenant.
4. No one shall be arbitrarily deprived of the right to enter his own country.

The Right to Freedom of Movement Within a Country, Which Includes the Right to Choose Where to Live Within the Country

People must be able to move freely and choose a place of residence within a country without restrictions, including establishing a purpose or reason for doing so. The only allowable restrictions are those mentioned in article 12(3) (see further detail below). Governments have a duty to ensure that a person's freedom of movement is not unduly restricted by others, including private persons or companies. The right applies to all persons lawfully within Australian territory, not only to Australian citizens.

International law does allow a country to impose restrictions on who may enter it. A country may allow entry to a non-citizen on conditions that allow the person lesser rights of freedom of movement to those of citizens, provided those restrictions comply with the country's international obligations. For example, some work visas impose conditions on a visa holder to reside and work in a particular region. However, a non-citizen lawfully within Australia whose entry into Australia has not been subject to restrictions or conditions is entitled to the same right to freedom of movement as an Australian citizen.

The Right to Leave Any Country, Regardless of Your Citizenship

The freedom to leave a country pertains to both short-term, long-term and permanent departures. It cannot be made dependent on establishing a purpose or reason for leaving. Citizens have a right to obtain passports or other travel documents from their country of citizenship. The right to leave, and to possess a passport, may be restricted, most notably if the person's presence is required due to their having been charged with a criminal offence.

The Right to Enter a Country of Which You Are a Citizen

The UN Human Rights Committee has stated that in no case may a person be arbitrarily deprived of the right to enter his or her own country, and that there are few, if any, circumstances in which deprivation of the right to enter a person's own country could be considered reasonable. This component of the right is generally restricted to citizens. Australian citizenship may be revoked by the Minister for Immigration and Citizenship in the circumstances set out in section 34 of the Australian Citizenship Act 2007. Complaints have been made to the UN Human Rights Committee by persons who have been ordered to leave countries in which they have been long-term residents, but not citizens, for example because they have committed serious criminal offences. The complaints have alleged that the country of long-term residence should be considered the person's 'own country'. So far, no such complaint has been successful, although individual members of the Committee have dissented from the views of the majority.

Limitations

This right can be restricted on any of the grounds in article 12(3) of the ICCPR, namely national security, public order, public health or morals, or the rights and freedoms of others. The Human Rights Committee has stated that restrictions should not only serve the permissible purposes; they must also be necessary and proportionate to protect them and must be the least intrusive means of achieving the desired result. Examples of measures likely to constitute permissible restrictions are those on persons charged with or convicted of criminal offences, access to areas of environmental significance, access to areas such as quarantine zones and prohibitions on unlicensed access to private premises, particularly where such access would interfere with the right to privacy of the owner or occupier of the premises.

In addition, Australia's obligations under the Hague Convention on the Civil Aspects of International Child Abduction provide an obligation on Australia to take measures to seek the return of children wrongfully removed or detained from their country of habitual residence. In fulfilling Australia's obligations under this and other conventions, Australian authorities are required to both actively prevent the wrongful removal of children from Australia and to actively seek the return of children who have been wrongfully removed.

Disability and Freedom of Movement

Freedom of movement needs to be available in practice as well as in law. The CRPD sets out in more detail the implications of this point including in Articles 9 and 20.

International Scrutiny

Nystrom v Australia (2011)
Deportation on character grounds (extensive record of serious criminal charges) of non-citizen who had lived almost all of his life in Australia. Committee (with 5 members dissenting) found breaches of ICCPR article 12.4. Discussion of concept of person's "own country".

Viewpoint 5

> *"The contracting states undertake to cooperate among themselves by taking all the measures that they may consider effective, under their own laws, and especially those established in this convention, to prevent and punish acts of terrorism, especially kidnaping, murder, and other assaults against the life or physical integrity of those persons."*

Transnational Repression Has Gotten Worse in Recent Decades

Organization of American States Department of International Law

The reason for revisiting this 1971 convention of the Organization of American States (OAS) is to show not only its stance against what is now called transnational repression but to show that the problem has actually worsened in modern times. The stand taken by the General Assembly of the OAS more than 50 years ago remains a beacon of morality against terrorism and persecution, but certainly did not prevent such acts by offending nations from continuing and even proliferating. The Organization of American States is a multilateral regional body focused on human rights, social and

"Convention to Prevent and Punish the Acts of Terrorism Taking the Form of Crimes Against Persons and Related Extortion that Are of International Significance/Third Special Session of the General Assembly, in Washington, D.C.," by Organization of American States/Department of International Law, February 2, 1971.

economic development, electoral oversight, and security throughout the Western hemisphere.

As you read, consider the following questions:

1. What crimes are addressed in this viewpoint?
2. According to the articles in this conviction, who is subject to extradition?
3. What obligations for countries are addressed in this viewpoint?

Signed at the Third Special Session of the General Assembly in Washington, D.C., February 2, 1971

Whereas:

The defense of freedom and justice and respect for the fundamental rights of the individual that are recognized by the American Declaration of the Rights and Duties of Man and the Universal Declaration of Human Rights are primary duties of states.

The General Assembly of the Organization, in Resolution 4, of June 30, 1970, strongly condemned acts of terrorism, especially the kidnaping of persons and extortion in connection with that crime, which it declared to be serious common crimes.

Criminal acts against persons entitled to special protection under international law are occurring frequently, and those acts are of international significance because of the consequences that may flow from them for relations among states.

It is advisable to adopt general standards that will progressively develop international law as regards cooperation in the prevention and punishment of such acts; and

In the application of those standards the institution of asylum should be maintained and, likewise the principle of nonintervention should not be impaired,

The Member States of the Organization of American States Have Agreed Upon the Following Articles:

Article 1

The contracting states undertake to cooperate among themselves by taking all the measures that they may consider effective, under their own laws, and especially those established in this convention, to prevent and punish acts of terrorism, especially kidnaping, murder, and other assaults against the life or physical integrity of those persons to whom the state has the duty according to international law to give special protection, as well as extortion in connection with those crimes.

Article 2

For the purposes of this convention, kidnaping, murder, and other assaults against the life or personal integrity of those persons to whom the state has the duty to give special protection according to international law, as well as extortion in connection with those crimes, shall be considered common crimes of international significance, regardless of motive.

Article 3

Persons who have been charged or convicted for any of the crimes referred to in Article 2 of this convention shall be subject to extradition under the provisions of the extradition treaties in force between the parties or, in the case of states that do not make extradition dependent on the existence of a treaty, in accordance with their own laws.

In any case, it is the exclusive responsibility of the state under whose jurisdiction or protection such persons are located to determine the nature of the acts and decide whether the standards of this convention are applicable.

Article 4

Any person deprived of his freedom through the application of this convention shall enjoy the legal guarantees of due process.

Article 5

When extradition requested for one of the crimes specified in Article 2 is not in order because the person sought is a national of the requested state, or because of some other legal or constitutional impediment, that state is obliged to submit the case to its competent authorities for prosecution, as if the act had been committed in its territory. The decision of these authorities shall be communicated to the state that requested extradition. In such proceedings, the obligation established in Article 4 shall be respected.

Article 6

None of the provisions of this convention shall be interpreted so as to impair the right of asylum.

Article 7

The contracting states undertake to include the crimes referred to in Article 2 of this convention among the punishable acts giving rise to extradition in any treaty on the subject to which they agree among themselves in the future. The contracting states that do not subject extradition to the existence of a treaty with the requesting state shall consider the crimes referred to in Article 2 of this convention as crimes giving rise to extradition, according to the conditions established by the laws of the requested state.

Article 8

To cooperate in preventing and punishing the crimes contemplated in Article 2 of this convention, the contracting states accept the following obligations:

- To take all measures within their power, and in conformity with their own laws, to prevent and impede the preparation in their respective territories of the crimes mentioned in Article 2 that are to be carried out in the territory of another contracting state.
- To exchange information and consider effective administrative measures for the purpose of protecting the persons to whom Article 2 of this convention refers.

- To guarantee to every person deprived of his freedom through the application of this convention every right to defend himself.
- To endeavor to have the criminal acts contemplated in this convention included in their penal laws, if not already so included.
- To comply most expeditiously with the requests for extradition concerning the criminal acts contemplated in this convention.

Article 9

This convention shall remain open for signature by the member states of the Organization of American States, as well as by any other state that is a member of the United Nations or any of its specialized agencies, or any state that is a party to the Statute of the International Court of Justice, or any other state that may be invited by the General Assembly of the Organization of American States to sign it.

Article 10

This convention shall be ratified by the signatory states in accordance with their respective constitutional procedures.

Article 11

The original instrument of this convention, the English, French, Portuguese, and Spanish texts of which are equally authentic, shall be deposited in the General Secretariat of the Organization of American States, which shall send certified copies to the signatory governments for purposes of ratification. The instruments of ratification shall be deposited in the General Secretariat of the Organization of American States, which shall notify the signatory governments of such deposit.

Article 12

This convention shall enter into force among the states that ratify it when they deposit their respective instruments of ratification.

Article 13

This convention shall remain in force indefinitely, but any of the contracting states may denounce it. The denunciation shall be transmitted to the General Secretariat of the Organization of American States, which shall notify the other contracting states thereof. One year following the denunciation, the convention shall cease to be in force for the denouncing state but shall continue to be in force for the other contracting states.

Statement of Panama

The Delegation of Panama states for the record that nothing in this convention shall be interpreted to the effect that the right of asylum implies the right to request asylum from the United States authorities in the Panama Canal Zone, or that there is recognition of the right of the United States to grant asylum or political refuge in that part of the territory of the Republic of Panama that constitutes the Canal Zone.

In witness whereof, the undersigned plenipotentiaries, having presented their full powers, which have been found to be in due and proper form, sign this convention on behalf of their respective governments, at the city of Washington this second day of February of the year one thousand none hundred seventy-one.

Periodical and Internet Sources Bibliography

The following articles have been selected to supplement the diverse views presented in this chapter.

"China: Draconian Repression of Muslims in Xinjiang Amounts to Crimes Against Humanity," Amnesty International, June 10, 2021. https://www.amnesty.org/en/latest/news/2021/06/china-draconian-repression-of-muslims-in-xinjiang-amounts-to-crimes-against-humanity/.

"Embassies and Transnational Repression," G.R. Berridge, May 25, 2021. "https://grberridge.diplomacy.edu/embassies-and-transnational-repression/.

"Governments Target Nationals Living Abroad: Killings, Removals, Other Abuses Threaten Rights; Bold Policy Response Needed," Human Rights Watch, February 22, 2024. https://www.hrw.org/news/2024/02/22/governments-target-nationals-living-abroad.

Lauren Baillie and Matthew Parkes, "Don't Look Away from China's Atrocities Against the Uyghurs," United States Institute of Peace, April 6, 2023. https://www.usip.org/publications/2023/04/dont-look-away-chinas-atrocities-against-uyghurs.

Marwa Fatafta, "Transnational Digital Repression in the MENA Region," Elliott School of International Affairs. https://pomeps.org/transnational-digital-repression-in-the-mena-region.

Marcus Michaelsen, "Special Report 2020: The Digital Transnational Repression Toolkit, and Its Silencing Effects," Freedom House. https://freedomhouse.org/report/special-report/2020/digital-transnational-repression-toolkit-and-its-silencing-effects.

Gissou Nia, "The US Needs Better Tools to Fight Transnational Repression. Here's Where to Start," Atlantic Council, July 29, 2021. https://www.atlanticcouncil.org/blogs/new-atlanticist/the-us-needs-better-tools-to-fight-transnational-repression-heres-where-to-start/.

Robert B. Smith, "Rebellion and Repression and the Vietnam War," the *Annals of the American Academy of Political and Social Science*, September 1970. https://www.jstor.org/stable/1040032.

Chapter 3

Are Extrajudicial Killings Common on the Global Stage?

Chapter Preface

The focus in Chapter 3 turns from transnational repression to extrajudicial killings, which certainly takes repression to the highest level. Extrajudicial killing is deliberate and unlawful killing without judicial process, including summary and arbitrary execution.

Among the examples cited here is the most publicized dissident murder of the modern era, that of Saudi journalist Jamal Khashoggi. His gruesome murder and dismemberment is discussed and debated in the first viewpoint of the chapter, which then goes on to other related subjects, such as the international community's tendency to ignore extrajudicial killings in the Middle East. These viewpoints examine how authoritarian regimes depend on extrajudicial killings to repress voices of dissent.

Also touched upon here is American history and the argument that it has historically been involved in extrajudicial killings within its own borders. One can claim the U.S. government practiced it in the 19th century with the destruction of the Native American culture and its people (including the Wounded Knee Massacre of 1890) and its citizens engaged in it with relative impunity during the Jim Crow era through lynchings of Black Americans.

Modern America is not immune to criticism. The police have been accused of extrajudicial killing in the highly publicized murders of Black motorists and others they confront. This chapter details those chapters of recent history and debates how those losses of life can be classified.

Readers of Chapter 3 can take a journey around the world through several issues related to extrajudicial killing and how the American and foreign governments seek to rationalize and even justify their actions. Accepting blame is a rare occurrence, especially among world leaders. It is up to their citizens such as the readers of these viewpoints to make logical, unbiased determinations.

Viewpoint 1

> *"Khashoggi's killing was internationally condemned and caused a diplomatic crisis between Saudi Arabia and some of its closest allies, including the U.S."*

Did Saudi Arabia Commit Extrajudicial Killing in the Murder of Jamal Khashoggi?

BBC News

Some have claimed that the Saudi government covered up its role in the murder of journalist Jamal Khashoggi in 2018 by holding a phony trial and making others the scapegoats for its own crime. They believe that the government held a trial only to sway public opinion about what was considered by many in the international community to be an extrajudicial killing perpetrated by its leaders. This viewpoint from BBC News details the trial, its outcome, and the reaction from the Saudis and others around the world. BBC News is a British public service broadcaster.

As you read, consider the following questions:

1. Who was Jamal Khashoggi and why would the Saudi government want to supress his opinions?
2. What actions did the Saudi government take in response to Khashoggi's murder?

"Jamal Khashoggi: All you need to know about Saudi journalist's death," BBC News, February 24, 2021. Reproduced with permission.

3. What did an investigation by the UN find about the killing?

On 2 October 2018, Jamal Khashoggi, a U.S.-based journalist and critic of Saudi Arabia's government, walked into the Saudi consulate in Istanbul, where he was murdered.

In the months that followed, conflicting narratives emerged over how he died, what happened to his remains, and who was responsible.

Saudi officials said the journalist was killed in a "rogue operation" by a team of agents sent to persuade him to return to the kingdom, while Turkish officials said the agents acted on orders from the highest levels of the Saudi government.

Who Was Jamal Khashoggi?

As a prominent Saudi journalist, he covered major stories, including the Soviet invasion of Afghanistan and the rise of the late al-Qaeda leader Osama Bin Laden, for various Saudi news organizations.

For decades, the 59-year-old was close to the Saudi royal family and also served as an adviser to the government.

But he fell out of favor and went into self-imposed exile in the U.S. in 2017. From there, he wrote a monthly column in the *Washington Post* in which he criticized the policies of Crown Prince Mohammed bin Salman, the son of King Salman and Saudi Arabia's de facto ruler.

In his first column for the *Post* in September 2017, Khashoggi said he had feared being arrested in an apparent crackdown on dissent overseen by the prince.

Why Was He at the Consulate?

Khashoggi first visited the Saudi consulate in Istanbul on 28 September 2018 to obtain a Saudi document stating that he was divorced, so that he could marry his Turkish fiancée, Hatice Cengiz.

But he was told he would have to return to pick up the document and arranged to come back on 2 October.

"He did not believe that something bad could happen on Turkish soil," Ms. Cengiz wrote in the Post.

Ms. Cengiz accompanied him to the entrance of the consulate on 2 October. He was last seen on CCTV footage entering the building at 13:14 local time.

Despite reassuring friends that he would not face any problems inside, he gave Ms. Cengiz two mobile phones and told her to call an adviser to Turkish President Recep Tayyip Erdogan if he did not come back out.

She ultimately waited for more than 10 hours outside the consulate and returned the following morning when Khashoggi had still not reappeared.

What Did Saudi Arabia Say?

For more than two weeks, Saudi Arabia consistently denied any knowledge of Khashoggi's fate.

Prince Mohammed told Bloomberg News that the journalist had left the consulate "after a few minutes or one hour". "We have nothing to hide," he added.

But in a change of tune on 20 October, the Saudi government said a preliminary investigation by prosecutors had concluded that the journalist died during a "fight" after resisting attempts to return him to Saudi Arabia. Later, a Saudi official attributed the death to a chokehold.

On 15 November, Saudi Arabia's deputy public prosecutor Shalaan al-Shalaan said the murder was ordered by the head of a "negotiations team" sent to Istanbul by the Saudi deputy intelligence chief to bring Khashoggi back to the kingdom "by means of persuasion" or, if that failed, "by force".

Investigators concluded that Khashoggi was forcibly restrained after a struggle and injected with a large amount of a drug, resulting in an overdose that led to his death, Mr. Shalaan said. His body was then dismembered and handed over to a local "collaborator" outside the consulate for disposal, he added.

Five individuals had confessed to the murder, Mr. Shalaan asserted, adding: "[The crown prince] did not have any knowledge about it."

What Actions Has Saudi Arabia Taken?

The Saudi public prosecution said in late September 2018 that a total of 31 individuals were investigated over the killing and that 21 of them were arrested.

Five senior government officials were also sacked, including Deputy Intelligence Chief Ahmad Asiri and Saud al-Qahtani, a senior aide to Prince Mohammed.

In January 2019, 11 individuals—who have not been named—were put on trial at the Riyadh Criminal Court in connection with Khashoggi's murder, and the public prosecutor sought the death penalty for five of them.

Human Rights Watch said the trial, which took place behind closed doors, did not meet international standards and that authorities "obstructed meaningful accountability".

In December 2019, the court sentenced five individuals to death for "committing and directly participating in the murder of the victim". Three others were handed prison sentences totaling 24 years for "covering up this crime and violating the law", while the remaining three were found not guilty.

The public prosecution said Mr. Asiri was tried but acquitted "due to insufficient evidence", while Mr. Qahtani was investigated over the killing but not charged.

At a news conference following the verdict, Shalaan al-Shalaan said the public prosecution's investigation had shown that "the killing was not premeditated".

Ms. Callamard dismissed that assertion as "utterly ridiculous" and said the trial represented "the antithesis of justice", from which the "masterminds" walked free.

But Khashoggi's son Salah, who lives in Saudi Arabia, tweeted: "We affirm our confidence in the Saudi judiciary at all levels, that it has been fair to us and that justice has been achieved."

In May 2020, Salah Khashoggi announced that he and his brothers were "pardoning those who killed our father, seeking reward from God almighty", accepting the public prosecution's contention that the murder was not premeditated.

Four months later, the Riyadh Criminal Court commuted the death sentences handed to five of the defendants to 20 years in prison. The three others were given sentences of between seven and 10 years. The prosecution said the verdicts were final and that the criminal trial was now closed.

Ms. Cengiz said the ruling made "a complete mockery of justice".

"The Saudi authorities are closing the case without the world knowing the truth of who is responsible for Jamal's murder," she added. "Who planned it, who ordered it, where is his body? These are the most basic and important questions that remain totally unanswered."

What Does Turkey Say Happened?

Turkish officials said that a team of 15 Saudi agents, assisted by three intelligence officers, arrived in Istanbul in the days before the murder, and that the group removed the security cameras and surveillance footage from the consulate before Khashoggi's arrival.

Istanbul's chief prosecutor, Irfan Fidan, said on 31 October 2018 that the journalist was suffocated almost as soon as entered the consulate, and that his body was dismembered and destroyed.

Writing in the *Washington Post* on 2 November, Turkish President Recep Tayyip Erdogan declared it had been established that Khashoggi "was killed in cold blood by a death squad" and "that his murder was premeditated".

"Yet there are other, no less significant questions whose answers will contribute to our understanding of this deplorable act" he added. "Where is Khashoggi's body? Who is the 'local collaborator' to whom Saudi officials claimed to have handed over Khashoggi's remains? Who gave the order to kill this kind soul? Unfortunately, the Saudi authorities have refused to answer those questions."

Mr. Erdogan said he knew the order to kill Khashoggi "came from the highest levels of the Saudi government", but that he did "not believe for a second that King Salman, the custodian of the holy mosques, ordered the hit".

In March 2020, the Istanbul chief prosecutor formally charged Saad al-Qahtani, Ahmad Asiri and 18 other Saudi nationals with murder.

Prince Mohammed's two former aides were accused of "instigating a premeditated murder with the intent of [causing] torment through fiendish instinct". The others were charged with carrying out "a premeditated murder with the intent of [causing] torment through fiendish instincts".

Saudi Arabia rejected Turkey's extradition request, so all 20 men were put on trial in absentia in Istanbul in July 2020. Court-appointed Turkish lawyers representing the defendants said their clients denied the charges.

In November, the court accepted a second indictment adding another six Saudis to the case. A vice-consul and an attaché were accused of "premeditated murder with monstrous intent". The four others were charged with destroying, concealing, or tampering with evidence.

What Did the UN Investigation Find?

A report released in June 2019 by Agnes Callamard, the special rapporteur, concluded that Khashoggi's death "constituted an extrajudicial killing for which the state of the Kingdom of Saudi Arabia is responsible".

She also found there was "credible evidence" to warrant an investigation into Prince Mohammed and other high-level Saudi officials and said the prince should be subject to the targeted sanctions already imposed by some UN member states against other named individuals allegedly involved in the killing.

Ms. Callamard said both the investigations into Khashoggi's death by Saudi Arabia and Turkey "failed to meet international standards".

She called for the trial in Saudi Arabia of the 11 suspects to be suspended, saying it would "not deliver credible accountability".

"The trial is held behind closed doors; the identity of those charged has not been released nor is the identity of those facing the death penalty. At the time of writing, at least one of those identified as responsible for the planning and organizing of the execution of Mr. Khashoggi has not been charged," she noted.

The Saudi Minister of State for Foreign Affairs, Adel al-Jubeir, rejected the report, tweeting that it was "nothing new" and contained "clear contradictions and baseless allegations which challenge its credibility".

"The Saudi judiciary is the sole party qualified to deal with the Khashoggi case and works with full independence," he added.

Is There Any Evidence?

In mid-November 2018, Turkey's government said it had shared audio recordings of the killing with Saudi Arabia, the U.S., the UK, Germany. and France. While not officially made public, details of the recordings were included in Ms. Callamard's report.

The UN special rapporteur noted that she was not able to obtain copies of the recordings from Turkish intelligence or authenticate them.

But in one recording, her report says, two Saudi officials are apparently heard discussing how to cut up and transport Khashoggi's body just minutes before the journalist entered the consulate.

One is quoted as saying: "The body is heavy. First time I cut on the ground. If we take plastic bags and cut it into pieces, it will be finished." At the end of the conversation, the other asks whether "the sacrificial animal" has arrived.

A later conversation recorded inside the consul general's office purportedly features Khashoggi being told by officials: "We will have to take you back. There is an order from Interpol. Interpol requested you to be sent back. We are coming to get you."

The reports quotes Khashoggi as replying that "there isn't a case against me. I notified some people outside; they are waiting for me; a driver is waiting for me."

At 13:33 local time, he is heard saying: "There is a towel here. Are you going to give me drugs?" Someone responds: "We will anaesthetize you."

The report says the conversation was followed by sounds of a struggle, during which people are heard saying, "Did he sleep?", "He raises his head," and "Keep pushing." Later, there are sounds of movement, heavy panting, and plastic sheets.

Turkish intelligence identified the sound of a saw at 13:39, but Ms. Callamard said she and her delegation could not make out the sources of the sounds they heard.

Assessments of the recordings by intelligence officers in Turkey and other countries suggest Khashoggi could have been injected with a sedative and then suffocated using a plastic bag, according to the special rapporteur.

Turkish officials were not granted access to the Saudi consulate for DNA testing until more than two weeks after the incident.

The special rapporteur said there was credible evidence that crime scenes had been "thoroughly, even forensically, cleaned" before investigators arrived.

Among the areas searched for Khashoggi's remains are the Belgrad forest, which a consular attaché visited on 1 October 2018, and the coastal town of Yalova, the location of a farmhouse allegedly owned by a Saudi national.

Who Are the Alleged Saudi Agents?

None of those put on trial have been identified by Saudi prosecutors, but the report by the UN special rapporteur named them, citing information from "various governments' sources".

According to the report, the five facing the death penalty were Fahad Shabib Albalawi; Turki Muserref Alshehri; Waleed Abdullah Alshehri; Maher Abdulaziz Mutreb, an intelligence officer who the U.S. says worked for the crowd prince's aide Saud al-Qahtani;

and Dr Salah Mohammed Tubaigy, a forensic doctor with the interior ministry.

The other six defendants were Mansour Othman Abahussain; Mohammed Saad Alzahrani; Mustafa Mohammed Almadani; Saif Saad Alqahtani; Muflih Shaya Almuslih, reportedly a member of the consulate staff; and Ahmad Asiri, the former deputy intelligence chief.

According to interviews conducted by the special rapporteur, the defendants' lawyers argued during a court hearing in January that they were "state employees and could not object to the orders of their superiors".

Three defendants allegedly said that Khashoggi "started screaming, so they covered his mouth to prevent him from making noise, which accidentally killed him", according to the report. Ms. Callamard noted that she had heard no screaming in the audio recordings from the consulate.

Mr.. Asiri was cited as telling the court that he had "never ordered the use of force" to bring Khashoggi back to Saudi Arabia.

Nine of the defendants named by Ms. Callamard were previously identified by Turkish officials as members of the 15-strong team of agents sent to Istanbul.

Most of the agents arrived at and departed from the city's airport by private or commercial jet the same day as Khashoggi's killing.

CCTV footage appears to show vehicles driving them to the consulate, and two hours after Khashoggi's arrival, some of them heading to the consul's residence.

The special rapporteur said three men were filmed entering the residence with what seemed like plastic trash bags, and at least one rolling suitcase.

How Have Saudi Arabia's Western Allies Reacted?

Khashoggi's killing was internationally condemned and caused a diplomatic crisis between Saudi Arabia and some of its closest allies, including the U.S.

After the murder was confirmed by the Saudis, then-U.S. President Donald Trump described it as the "worst cover-up in history". However, he defended U.S. ties to the kingdom, a key trading partner.

This response was widely derided by senators in Congress, who pointed the finger at Prince Mohammed.

According to U.S. media reports, the CIA—whose director heard the consulate audio recordings—concluded with "medium to high confidence" that Prince Mohammed ordered Khashoggi's killing.

Mr. Trump denied that and his administration defied a legal requirement to release an unclassified report identifying anyone implicated in "the directing, ordering or tampering of evidence" in the case. His successor, Joe Biden, has said he will declassify the report.

The U.S., Canada, France, and the UK all levied sanctions against 18 Saudis allegedly linked to the killing. The Saudi crown prince was not among them.

Germany, Finland, and Denmark were among the European nations to cancel arms deals with Saudi Arabia after the killing.

VIEWPOINT 2

> *"If anything positive came out of the tragic murder of Khashoggi, it is that there has finally been extensive global media attention given to an extrajudicial killing in the diaspora."*

Jamal Khashoggi's Murder Shows the World the Dangers Exiled Dissidents Face

Sahar Khamis

As the previous viewpoint indicated, the murder of Jamal Khashoggi raised attention around the world about the issue of extrajudicial killings of dissidents by some Middle Eastern nations. As Sahar Khamis explains in this viewpoint, that murder was very high profile, but it was far from the first one. Since the protest movements that occurred in various Middle Eastern countries during the Arab Spring of 2011, many of these countries—as well as others in the region—have become more repressive in order to maintain authoritarian control. Many of the extrajudicial killings of cyberactivists and other dissidents that have occurred went largely unacknowledged, but Khashoggi's murder had the potential to mark a turning point. Sahar Khamis is an associate professor of communication at the University of Maryland.

"Jamal Khashoggi's Murder Finally Brings Media Attention to Plight of Arab World's Exiled Critics," by Sahar Khamis, The Conversation, November 2, 2018, https://theconversation.com/jamal-khashoggis-murder-finally-brings-media-attention-to-plight-of-arab-worlds-exiled-critics-105705.

As you read, consider the following questions:

1. Which countries were involved in the Arab Spring of 2011?
2. In what ways is Saudi Arabia a paradox, according to Khamis?
3. Why do the people who live in these countries accept repression, according to this viewpoint?

The gruesome and dramatic killing of journalist Jamal Khashoggi in the Saudi consulate in Turkey has captivated media outlets around the world.

A columnist for the *Washington Post*, Khashoggi had been living in the United States since 2017 as a Saudi exile.

Some have frowned upon this excessive coverage, wondering why one particular instance of Saudi butchery was making headlines, while the Saudi-backed war in Yemen has been going on for years, has claimed the lives of thousands of children and hasn't received a fraction of the attention.

But I think the coverage of Khashoggi's murder is important. As an expert in Arab media, I've studied the cyberactivists who work to bring about political and social change in the Arab world.

For the first time, the media is bringing widespread attention to the real dangers faced every day by opponents of Arab regimes living abroad.

This was not the first, nor will it be the last, government-orchestrated crime against Arab journalists and activists who are living in exile. However, before Khashoggi's death, many of these crimes went unnoticed or underreported.

The Arab Spring Fizzles—and Many Flee

Beginning in 2011, waves of opposition to the regimes in power swept through six Arab countries: Tunisia, Libya, Egypt, Yemen, Syria, and Bahrain.

Known as the Arab Spring, many of these protest movements had a similar set of demands: freedom, dignity, and democracy.

Some of these countries were long led by dictators, such as Hosni Mubarak, who ruled Egypt for 30 years; Moammar Gadhafi, who ruled Libya for 42 years; and Zine El Abidine Ben Ali, who ruled Tunisia for 23 years. It was the first time in decades that these countries witnessed popular uprisings that shook the thrones of political leaders and ousted them from power.

Tunisia was able to chart a relatively smooth, peaceful path toward reform and democratization.

But it ended up being the exception.

The rest of the Arab Spring countries had brief dalliances with democracy, only to revert to a system of political oppression and authoritarianism.

Today, Libya is torn by sectarian strife; Yemen is being bombed day and night; Syria is experiencing the worst civil war in modern history; Egypt returned to a military dictatorship far worse than Mubarak's; and Bahrain's uprising was suppressed.

Fearing for their lives and safety—and unable to openly organize and express themselves—many of the leading Arab Spring activists and journalists fled their home countries.

Some, such as Egyptian blogger Wael Abbas, didn't make it out and remain imprisoned in their home countries. Others, such as Egyptian blogger Maikel Nabil Sanad, are now living in exile.

Although Saudi Arabia wasn't officially one of the Arab Spring countries, anti-government protests did crop up across the nation in 2011 and 2012. There was enough concern among the ruling class to further crack down and suppress opposing voices.

The heightened repression and stifling of freedom of expression in Saudi Arabia forced many dissidents and opponents to flee the country and, like their Arab Spring peers, exercise their opposition in the diaspora.

For many years, Jamal Khashoggi worked as a journalist in Saudi Arabia, eventually becoming editor-in-chief of the Saudi

Arabian daily *al-Watan*. But in 2003, authorities removed him from his position after one of his columnists wrote a piece critical of an Islamic scholar. Khashoggi moved to London, bounced around the Middle East, and regularly wrote for the Dubai-based periodical *al-Arabiya*.

The U.S. Has Also Committed Extrajudicial Killings in the Middle East

On 29 August 2021 just days before the U.S. withdrawal from Afghanistan, a drone strike killed 10 civilians of one family. The target was an innocent aid worker and his family members, including seven children. The U.S. merely acknowledged the mistakes, and according to a BBC report, described the strike as a "tragic mistake" only.

Last year, Tariq Aziz, another 16-year-old boy, a soccer player, also died when a drone strike lit up his car in Pakistan. Since the last decade, the U.S. drone strike has caused numerous casualties worldwide, including in Pakistan, Yemen, Somalia, and Afghanistan. According to the Bureau of Investigative journalism statistics, since 2004, drone strikes in Yemen have killed at least 174-225 civilians, with total death of 1020-1389. In Pakistan, the number is even worse. According to the Bureau of Investigative journalism statistics, drone strikes killed 2500-4000 people, including 424-969 civilians in Pakistan.

The events and unfortunate stories are only a glimpse of the USA's extrajudicial killings, its practice of targeted killings, and violations of human rights internationally. It seems, in the name of national security and war against terror, the "champion of human rights' is continuously violating human rights and bypassing international laws and norms for decades.

continued on next spread

Targeted Killings

According to a Foreign Policy article by American professor Charli Carpenter, targeted killing is a clear violation of human rights. Target listing or making a 'Kill list' is also a violation of basic tenets. There are international prohibitions on this issue. But it seems, since 9/11, the current hegemon—the USA itself is breaching these laws daily.

However, this is not the only prohibition the USA has breached. The drone strike on Iranian military commander Qasem Soleimani on Jan 3, 2020, also violated international laws related to internationally protected persons. As an official of the Iran government, Soleimani was an internationally protected person. Therefore, killing Soleimani is a violation of international laws and norms.

Apart from international laws and norms, targeted killing is also an act of 'extrajudicial killings,' and it overrides due legal process and 'right to justice'.

"US extrajudicial killings and 'Western Immorality'" by Ahmad Faraz. South Asia Monitor, Oct 12, 2021.

An Attack on One, an Attack on All

While Khashoggi eventually relocated to the U.S. in 2017, many political bloggers and activists who oppose Arab ruling regimes have moved to Turkey.

Dr. Ayman Nour, for example, was arrested in Egypt in 2005 for daring to run as a presidential candidate against former President Hosni Mubarak. After the military coup in Egypt in 2013, Nour founded al-Sharq, a Turkey-based opposition TV channel, which aims to expose the repression and authoritarianism of the current Egyptian regime.

Shaken by Khashoggi's murder, he and a number of prominent Arab and Turkish figures created the group "Jamal Khashoggi Friends Association" to raise international awareness about this hideous crime and the alarming message it sends to other opponents of autocratic regimes.

To activists like Nour, the attack on Khashoggi is an attack on everyone in the Arab opposition movement in the diaspora.

Unfortunately, their safety in their host countries has been far from guaranteed. In recent years, there have been a number of tragic incidents of violence and aggression directed at some of these activists.

Last year, Ahmed Barakat broke into the Istanbul apartment of his cousin, Syrian opposition activist Orouba Barakat, and her daughter, Halla Barakat, a journalist who worked for the Syrian opposition channel Orient News TV, and gruesomely slaughtered both of them. Many suspect that Ahmed Barakat, a former Free Syrian Army fighter, had been directed by the Assad regime to carry out the murders.

In March of this year, Saudi women's rights activist Loujain al-Hathloul was plucked from the streets of Abu Dhabi by security forces who returned her to Saudi Arabia, where she remains imprisoned.

After Khashoggi's murder, I reached out to a Syrian-American journalist living in exile in the United States, but who has contact with people in Turkey. Due to safety concerns, she spoke with me under condition of anonymity.

She noted that "especially after Khashoggi's murder…the Turkish government [has] adopted tougher security measures." But his death was only the latest. "Several Syrian opposition figures have been previously targeted and killed in Turkey," she added.

Saudi Opposition Weak at Home and Abroad

Why aren't the loudest voices opposing Khashoggi's murder Saudi ones?

The country is, in many ways, a paradox.

On one hand, it has a very large, young, tech-savvy population and is the country with the fourth-largest number of Twitter users in the world.

On the other hand, however, there's no freedom of the press, and public debate is pretty much nonexistent.

This explains why there has been complete silence inside Saudi Arabia around Khashoggi's death aside from the ruling regime's narrative, which has evolved from denial, to evasion, to partial confession.

While there has been a growing movement of Saudi opposition in the diaspora, unlike the Egyptian and Syrian opposition movements, which have been more organized and capable of creating their own associations, Saudi opponents remain few and far between. They are mostly young activists using their social media platforms to voice individual criticisms.

One such activist is Omar Abdulaziz. A friend of Khashoggi's, the young Saudi dissident lives in Montreal, Canada.

Using his YouTube, Twitter, and Instagram accounts, Omar is openly critical of the Saudi regime for its repression, corruption, and human rights violations.

His vocal opposition hasn't gone unpunished. In August 2018, the Saudi regime arrested two of his brothers and some of his friends in an act of retaliation. Yet, Omar has insisted that he won't be silenced, intimidated, or blackmailed.

Following Khashoggi's murder, Omar described the Saudi crown prince as an "illegitimate leader" and a "killer" on Twitter and YouTube.

Because the price of activism—even abroad—can be so high, the public-facing Abdulaziz is an exception. Most Saudi opponents will keep a much lower profile, using pseudonyms or posting anonymously.

What Happens Next?

Authoritarian Arab regimes have tightened their grip on power and escalated their mechanisms of repression in the years since the Arab Spring uprisings.

Many of these regimes have been enabled by their own people, many of whom are either apathetic or supportive of their repressive policies: They prioritize the promise of stability over the dream of freedom.

They've also been emboldened by the current American administration, which practices a brand of realpolitik that prioritizes its economic interests over its values when dealing with autocrats and dictators.

But the death of Arab opponents such as Jamal Khashoggi doesn't signal the death of Arab opposition.

With the whole world watching, texting, tweeting and chatting, I believe that many of these governments will eventually be condemned in the court of public opinion, both at home and abroad.

If anything positive came out of the tragic murder of Khashoggi, it is that there has finally been extensive global media attention given to an extrajudicial killing in the diaspora.

The Saudi regime might think twice about trying to pull off something similar.

Viewpoint 3

> *"The history that society colludes to avoid publicly is necessarily remembered privately."*

Was the Tulsa Race Massacre an Example of Extrajudicial Killing in the U.S.?

Gregory B. Fairchild

The United States has a tragic history of lynchings, primarily of Black Americans, beginning with the pre-Civil War era and lasting into the civil rights movement of the 1950s and 1960s. These lynchings were extrajudicial killings, and among these examples was the Tulsa race massacre of 1921. During this event, mobs of white residents in Tulsa, Oklahoma, destroyed the homes and businesses of Black residents and killed and injured many of them. This event was an egregious example of the extrajudicial killings many Black Americans faced in the form of lynching, but it goes largely undiscussed in conversations about American history. Acknowledgement of the atrocities that have occurred are essential for righting these wrongs. Gregory B. Fairchild is an associate professor of business administration at the University of Virginia.

As you read, consider the following questions:

1. According to the article from the *Washington Post* cited in this viewpoint, what is the estimated number of deaths that occurred during the Tulsa race massacre?
2. When did the city of Tulsa formally acknowledge that these events had occurred?
3. How does Fairchild believe historical wrongs can be corrected?

When Viola Fletcher, 107, appeared before Congress in May 2021, she called for the nation to officially acknowledge the Tulsa race riot of 1921.

I know that place and year well. As is the case with Fletcher—who is one of the last living survivors of the massacre, which took place when she was 7—the terror of the Tulsa race riot is something that has been with me for almost as long as I can remember. My grandfather, Robert Fairchild, told the story nearly a quarter-century ago to several newspapers.

Here's how *The Washington Post* recounted his story in 1996:

> At 92 years old, Robert Fairchild is losing his hearing, but he can still make out the distant shouts of angry white men firing guns late into the night 75 years ago. His eyes are not what they used to be, but he has no trouble seeing the dense, gray smoke swallowing his neighbors' houses as he walked home from a graduation rehearsal, a frightened boy of 17.
>
> His has since been a life of middle-class comfort, a good job working for the city, a warm family life. But he has never forgotten his mother's anguish in 1921 as she fled toward the railroad tracks to escape the mobs and fires tearing through the vibrant Black neighborhood of Greenwood in north Tulsa.

"There was just nothing left," Fairchild told the newspaper.

The Washington Post article said the Tulsa race riots of 1921 were among the "worst race riots in the nation's history." It reported: "The death toll during the 12-hour rampage is still in dispute, but estimates have put it as high as 250. More than 1,000 businesses and homes were burned to the ground, scores of Black families were herded into cattle pens at the fairgrounds, and one of the largest and most prosperous Black communities in the United States was turned to ashes."

Riots began after a white mob attempted to lynch a teenager falsely accused of assaulting a white woman. Black residents came to his defense, some armed. The groups traded shots, and mob violence followed. My family eventually returned to a decimated street. Miraculously their home on Latimer Avenue was spared.

Disturbing History

Hearing about these experiences at the family table was troubling enough. Reading a newspaper account of your ancestors' fleeing for their lives is a surreal pain. There's recognition of your family's terror, and relief in knowing your family survived what "60 Minutes" once called "one of the worst race massacres in American history."

In spite of my grandfather's witness, this same event didn't merit inclusion in any of my assigned history texts, either in high school or college. On the occasions I've mentioned this history to my colleagues, they've been astonished.

In 1996, at the 75th anniversary of the massacre, the city of Tulsa finally acknowledged what had happened. Community leaders from different backgrounds publicly recognized the devastation wrought by the riots. They gathered in a church that had been torched in the riot and since rebuilt. My grandfather told *The New York* Times then that he was "extremely pleased that Tulsa has taken this occasion seriously."

"A mistake has been made," he told the paper, "and this is a way to really look at it, then look toward the future and try to make sure it never happens again."

That it took so long for the city to acknowledge what took place shows how selective society can be when it comes to which historical events it chooses to remember—and which ones to overlook. The history that society colludes to avoid publicly is necessarily remembered privately.

Economically Vibrant

Even with massive destruction, the area of North Tulsa, known as Greenwood, became known for its economic vitality. On the blocks surrounding the corner of Archer Street and Greenwood Avenue in the 1930s, a thriving business district flourished with retail shops, entertainment venues, and high-end services. One of these businesses was the *Oklahoma Eagle*, a Black-owned newspaper. As a teenager in the early 1940s, my father had his first job delivering the paper.

Without knowing the history, it would be a surprise to the casual observer that years earlier everything in this neighborhood had been razed to the ground. The Black Wall Street Memorial, a black marble monolith, sits outside the Greenwood Cultural Center. The memorial is dedicated to the entrepreneurs and pioneers who made Greenwood Avenue what it was both before and after it was destroyed in the 1921 riot.

Although I grew up on military bases across the world, I would visit Greenwood many times over the years. As I grew into my teenage years in the 1970s, I recognized that the former vibrant community was beginning to decline. Some of this was due to the destructive effects of urban renewal and displacement. As with many other Black communities across the country, parts of Greenwood were razed to make way for highways.

Some of the decline was due to the exit of financial institutions, including banks. This contributed to a decrease in opportunities to build wealth, including savings and investment products, loans for homes and businesses, and funding to help build health clinics and affordable housing.

And at least some was due to the diminished loyalty of residents to Black-owned businesses and institutions. During the civil rights movement, downtown Tulsa businesses began to allow Black people into their doors as customers. As a result, Black residents spent less money in their community.

Historical Lessons

At the end of my father's military career in the 1970s, he became a community development banker in Virginia. His work involved bringing together institutions—investors, financial institutions, philanthropists, local governments—to develop innovative development solutions for areas like Greenwood. For me, there are lessons in the experiences of three generations—my grandfather's, father's, and mine—that influence my scholarly work today.

On the one hand, I study how years after the end of legal segregation Americans remain racially separate in our neighborhoods, schools and workplaces and at alarmingly high levels. My research has shown how segregation depresses economic and social outcomes. In short, segregation creates closed markets that stunt economic activity, especially in the Black community.

On the other hand, I focus on solutions. One avenue of work involves examining the business models of Community Development Financial Institutions, or CDFIs, and Minority Depository Institutions, or MDIs. These are financial institutions that are committed to economic development—banks, credit unions, loan funds, equity funds—that operate in low- and moderate-income neighborhoods. They offer what was sorely needed in North Tulsa, and many other neighborhoods across the nation—locally attuned financial institutions that understand the unique challenges families and businesses face in minority communities.

Righting Historical Wrongs

There are interventions we can take, locally and nationally, that recognize centuries of financial and social constraint. Initiatives like the 2020 decision by the Small Business Administration and U.S. Treasury to allocate US$10 billion to lenders that focus funds on disadvantaged areas are a start. These types of programs are needed even when there aren't full-scale economic and social crises are taking place, like the COVID-19 epidemic or protesters in the street. Years of institutional barriers and racial wealth gaps cannot be redressed unless there's a recognition that capital matters.

The 1921 Tulsa race riot began on May 31, only weeks before the annual celebration of Juneteenth, which is observed on June 19. As communities across the country begin recognizing Juneteenth and leading corporations move to celebrate it, it's important to remember the story behind Juneteenth—slaves weren't informed that they were emancipated.

After the celebrations, there's hard work ahead. From my grandfather's memory of the riot's devastation to my own work addressing low-income communities' economic challenges, I have come to see that change requires harnessing economic, governmental and nonprofit solutions that recognize and speak openly about the significant residential, educational and workplace racial segregation that still exists in the United States today.

Viewpoint 4

> *"[The] masking of religious practices did not stop the U.S. government from using violence to suppress these Native American ceremonies."*

The U.S. Used Violence to Religiously Suppress Native Americans

Rosalyn R. LaPier

In this viewpoint Rosalyn R. LaPier references a 2019 incident in which then-President Donald Trump made a joke about the Wounded Knee massacre of 1890. LaPier discusses how the U.S. government suppressed the religious beliefs and practices of Native Americans up until the 20th century. She also explains that religious suppression plays a role in the Wounded Knee massacre, in which hundreds of unarmed Native American men, women, and children were killed by the U.S. military while performing a religious ceremony. It took many years for the rights of American Indians to be acknowledged and protected, and inaccurately portraying devastating incidents like the Wounded Knee massacre does not help support this goal. Rosalyn R. LaPier is a professor of history at the University of Illinois at Urbana-Champaign.

As you read, consider the following questions:

1. Why were Indigenous practices not considered religious by many Americans before the 20th century?
2. How did Native American groups try to convince government agents to allow them to perform their religious ceremonies?
3. What legislation was passed to protect the religious rights of Native Americans and when was this passed?

President Trump evoked the Wounded Knee massacre in a recent tweet. He was reacting to an Instagram video that Sen. Elizabeth Warren posted on New Year's Eve.

> If Elizabeth Warren, often referred to by me as Pocahontas, did this commercial from Bighorn or Wounded Knee instead of her kitchen, with her husband dressed in full Indian garb, it would have been a smash!

There's been considerable criticism of the president's inaccurate portrayal of Native American history, including from members of his own party. Two Republican senators from South Dakota, Mike Rounds and John Thune, spoke out against the tweet.

Wounded Knee is among the worst massacres in Native American history. It was also one of the most violent examples of the repression of indigenous religion in American history.

Religious Suppression

Religion historian Tisa Wenger explains that before the 20th century, many Americans believed that "indigenous practices were by definition savage, superstitious, and coercive." They did not consider them to be religion.

In part because of this belief, the U.S. government decided not to recognize Native Americans as citizens of sovereign governments in the 19th century, but as colonial subjects. In 1883, the Department of Interior enacted the first "Indian Religious

Crimes Code" making the practice of Native American religions illegal. These codes remained in place until 1934.

In response, Wenger writes, some Native American groups tried to convince government agents that their gatherings were places of "prayer and worship" similar to Christian churches. Others claimed that their gathering were "social," not religious.

But this kind of masking of religious practices did not stop the U.S. government from using violence to suppress these Native American ceremonies.

In 1890, the U.S. military shot and killed hundreds of unarmed men, women and children at Wounded Knee, South Dakota, in an effort to suppress a Native American religious ceremony called the "ghost dance."

Historian Louis Warren explains that the ghost dance developed as a religious practice in the late 19th century after Native Americans witnessed the devastating environmental change of their homelands from American settlement. The dance envisioned a return to their unspoiled natural world.

The U.S. military, however, viewed it differently. They believed the Native Americans at Wounded Knee were gathering for war.

The Darkest Moment

The U.S. government changed its policies of openly suppressing indigenous religions in 1934. But it would take another 44 years before the U.S. fully committed "to protect and preserve" religious rights of American Indians through the American Indian Religious Freedom Act in 1978.

As a Native American scholar of religion and environment history, I agree with Republican Sen. Mike Rounds – the Wounded Knee massacre "should never be used as a punchline."

Periodical and Internet Sources Bibliography

The following articles have been selected to supplement the diverse views presented in this chapter.

"Extrajudicial Killing of Black Americans," Center for Justice and Accountability. https://cja.org/what-we-do/litigation/extrajudicial-killing-of-black-americans/.

"Saudi Arabia: Still No Justice for State-Sanctioned Murder of Jamal Khashoggi Five Years On," Amnesty International, September 29, 2023. https://www.amnesty.org/en/latest/news/2023/09/saudi-arabia-still-no-justice-for-state-sanctioned-murder-of-jamal-khashoggi-five-years-on/.

"Third Committee Experts Call for Stronger Laws to Uproot Legacies of Colonialism, Tackle Extrajudicial Killings Fueled by Racism as Delegates Support Prosecution," United Nations, October 26, 2021. https://press.un.org/en/2021/gashc4331.doc.htm.

William Aceves, "When Death Becomes Murder: A Primer on Extrajudicial Killing," *Columbia Human Rights Law Review*. https://hrlr.law.columbia.edu/hrlr/when-death-becomes-a-murder-a-primer-on-extrajudicial-killing/.

Kevin K. Gaines, "Global Black Lives Matter," *American Quarterly*, September 2022. https://muse.jhu.edu/pub/1/article/865417/summary.

Andrew Scobell, "What China Wants in the Middle East," United States Institute of Peace, November 1, 2023. https://www.usip.org/publications/2023/11/what-china-wants-middle-east.

Udi Sommer and Asal Victor, "Examining Extrajudicial Killings: Discriminant Analyses of Human Rights Violations," *Dynamics of Asymmetric Conflict*, June 2019. https://www.tandfonline.com/doi/abs/10.1080/17467586.2019.1622026.

Amanda L.M. van Rij, "Jamal Khashoggi: Why the US is Unlikely to Deliver Justice for the Murdered Journalist," The Conversation, March 2, 2021. https://theconversation.com/jamal-khashoggi-why-the-us-is-unlikely-to-deliver-justice-for-the-murdered-journalist-156165.

Chapter 4

Can Transnational Repression and Extrajudicial Killings Be Punished and Prevented?

Chapter Preface

Chapter 4 casts an eye to the future and how the present is creating a path to it. It was famously stated that those who do not learn from history are doomed to repeat it.

Morally sound world leaders and organizations that deal with transnational repression and extrajudicial killings are attempting to learn from history to end such terrible practices in the future. Unfortunately, "bad actors" on the world stage are doing the same thing in an attempt to increase and make more effective use of transnational repression and extrajudicial killing.

Who will win this power struggle? This chapter again studies both the proven and possible future influence—or lack thereof—of transnational bodies like the United Nations (UN), the International Criminal Court (ICC), and the International Court of Justice (ICJ, which is also part of the UN). Can the UN shed its growing reputation as ineffectual and band countries together in a common goal to end or at least limit such tactics? Can it create or become involved in positive diplomacy? Are the UN, ICJ, and ICC simply too limited in their power to influence superpowers such as the United States, Russia, and China? Is the Middle East too turbulent for these bodies to reduce tensions?

A strong focus in this chapter is also on potential U.S. response to transnational repression and extrajudicial killings. The Transnational Repression Policy Act has been introduced and debated in Congress but has not been passed into law as of 2024. One viewpoint discusses what actions the U.S. government could take to effectively address transnational repression. Another viewpoint in this chapter cites the failures of other tactics against offending nations. It suggests that sanctions simply do not work against dictatorships such as China that, according to the Committee on Homeland Security, is responsible for 30 percent of all transnational repression on the world stage.

Nothing can be done about the past. But the world can learn from it. What are the best potential solutions moving forward? These viewpoints will help readers decide.

Viewpoint 1

> *"The UN's inability to respond appropriately to the war in Ukraine is more an indicator than a trigger of the crisis of multilateralism."*

Does the UN Lack Power on the International Stage?

Monica Herz and Giancarlo Summa

In this viewpoint Monica Herz and Giancarlo Summa discuss the role of the United Nations in addressing contemporary issues. The UN has historically helped create a sense of multilateralism in which the global community accepts a certain set of norms and standards while institutionalizing cooperation and coordination. However, according to the authors there has been a crisis in multilateralism in the UN's response to conflicts and human rights violations like Russia's invasion of Ukraine. Nowadays the multilateral system is more focused on the power struggle between global superpowers like the U.S. and China, leaving the concerns of other countries and endangered populations ignored. Monica Herz is a professor at the Institute of International Relations (PUC-Rio), Associate Dean for Research of the Social Science Center (PUC-Rio), and a senior researcher BRICS Policy Center of the Pontifícia Universidade Católica do Rio de Janeiro (PUC-Rio). Giancarlo Summa is

"The UN and the Multilateral System Are in Crisis—What the Global South Must Do," by Monica Herz and Giancarlo Summa, The Conversation, September 28, 2023, https://theconversation.com/the-un-and-the-multilateral-system-are-in-crisis-what-the-global-south-must-do-214515.

cofounder of the MUDRAL project (Multilateralism and Radical Right in Latin America). Both are based in Brazil.

As you read, consider the following questions:

1. When was the UN created, and what was its purpose?
2. When did the trend of decreasing numbers of conflicts and victims begin to reverse?
3. According to the authors, what is the issue with the UN treating all states equally?

The planet is on fire, but almost all the firefighters have deserted. At the meeting of the United Nations General Assembly, which began on September 19 in New York, the leaders of four of the five permanent members of the Security Council—the UN's most powerful executive body—were absent.

The absence of the top representatives of France, the United Kingdom, Russia, and China, replaced by ministers or diplomats, demonstrated the emptying of the main global multilateral forum and highlighted the speeches of the two presidents who opened the General Assembly: Brazil's Luiz Inácio Lula da Silva and the U.S.'s Joe Biden.

Both leaders, with decades of experience, referred bluntly to fires that are ravaging the planet—starting with the climate emergency and the war in Ukraine. And both, albeit in very different tones, pointed the finger at the central issue hanging over the meeting, which the absentees made clear: the crisis of the UN and the multilateral system that has been built around it in recent decades.

The UN was created in 1945, on the initiative of the United States and with the support of the allied countries that had defeated Nazism and fascism (primarily the Soviet Union, Great Britain, and France) with the aim of "preserving future generations from the scourge of war".

A year earlier, in 1944, the Bretton Woods Agreements had laid the foundations for the post-war global financial system, and created the World Bank and the International Monetary Fund. Over the years, dozens of agencies, funds and specialised programmes have been added, gradually building up what is known as the UN System.

Practically every country in the world is a member of the UN and the organisation deals with countless issues, ranging from protecting life in the oceans to coordinating satellite orbits, humanitarian aid operations, vaccination campaigns, agreements to limit climate change, and, more recently, attempts to create regulations against disinformation on social networks and to combat tax avoidance by large international corporations.

An Imperfect System, but One that Worked

The system, as Biden pointed out in his speech, "is not always perfect and has not always been perfect", but with its ups and downs, it worked reasonably well for seven decades. During the Cold War, the UN was a crucial channel of communication that contributed to avoiding nuclear conflict. After it, the UN's remit expanded further: for example, with the multiplication of peacekeeping operations.

Despite the genocide in Rwanda, the civil war in the former Yugoslavia, and the invasion of Iraq in 2003, in those two decades the number of armed conflicts (between countries and within countries) steadily declined, as did the number of victims. The curve reversed in 2012, when the civil war in Syria worsened, and since then it has continued to rise year on year. According to the Conflict Data Programme at Uppsala University, 184 different conflicts were recorded in 2022, including the war in Ukraine, with more than 238,000 victims in total, compared to an average of 120 conflicts and 30,000 victims per year between 2001 and 2012.

The UN's inability to respond appropriately to the war in Ukraine is more an indicator than a trigger of the crisis of multilateralism. Russia has brought the war of aggression, of territorial annexation, back as a tool of foreign policy. But the same Western powers with permanent seats on the Security Council that are rightly criticising the Russian invasion today have resorted to the unilateral use of military force in recent decades, contrary to the UN Charter and international law.

What we usually call multilateralism is the way in which the international system adopts a grammar of principles and norms that, in theory, should be followed by all states. It is a process of institutionalising forms of coordination and cooperation in public policy that generates a certain stability and predictability in relations between states and societies.

In the way the UN works, there is an element of equality in the treatment of states (all 193 member countries have the right to vote and voice in the General Assembly), but there are also obvious asymmetries of power, such as the special status of the five permanent members of the Security Council. The so-called P5 have kept their veto power unchanged since 1945 and often ignore the rules they are supposed to enforce—a historical incongruity that Lula rightly attacked again in his speech in New York.

Global Governance

Even so, this grammar organises a large part of global governance mechanisms, which increase international dialogue and cooperation, and decrease the propensity to use force as the main instrument for settling disputes.

The UN system is based on the idea that power relations between states should not be the only element that determines the shape of international relations. In fact, as recently as 2015, the multilateral system reached a consensus to adopt two global agreements of great importance and impact: the Paris Agreement for the reduction of greenhouse gases, responsible for the climate emergency, and the Agenda 2030 for sustainable development.

From then on, the multilateral system was able to do little more than try to manage a growing number of humanitarian emergencies. In June 2023, the UN Office for the Coordination of Humanitarian Assistance (OCHA) estimated that there were 362 million people around the world in need of international aid to meet their basic survival needs.

A Crisis of Legitimacy and Authority

During the COVID-19 pandemic, the World Health Organization, under heavy fire from the administration of then U.S. President Donald Trump, was virtually ignored by the richest countries in its attempt to ensure equitable distribution of vaccines. The conflicts in Syria, Yemen, and Israel/Palestine drag on, with no solution in sight. Efforts to strengthen the UN's capacity for preventive diplomacy, promised by Secretary-General António Guterres, have backfired, and the organisation has been unable to do anything to prevent the invasion of Ukraine or to facilitate a ceasefire. The system has apparently ground to a halt.

It continues to shape a large part of international interaction, but today there are two key areas of resistance to it: the emergence of countries in the Global South willing to reinterpret the hegemony of the liberal order, and the growth of a transnationally articulated radical right.

In the international debate, there is much more attention paid to the first question than the second. However, as the experience of the Trump and Bolsonaro governments has shown, the radical right's sovereigntist vision is at odds with the essence of multilateralism, which requires agreed transfers of national sovereignty in favour of common goals, such as the fight against climate change. It's no coincidence that the Spanish radical right party Vox has been running a campaign against the 2030 Agenda for years, which has been expanding throughout Latin America. Even so, the entire UN bureaucracy, from Secretary-General Guterres onwards, is reluctant to engage in open conflict with the radical right.

A Strategic Problem

For Brazil, and Latin America in general, the crisis of the multilateral system is a strategic problem. The region has an old multilateralist tradition, in which conflicts between states have been resolved by diplomatic means and not by arms. A dozen countries from the region took part in the creation of the League of Nations in 1920, and 20 were among the 51 founding nations of the UN. To this day, the multilateral space represents the only international arena in which the region has any influence, since from an economic and military point of view Latin America's weight is extremely limited: the region is home to 8 percent of the world's population, but in 2022 it accounted for only 5.26 percent of global GDP.

At the same time, the collective influence of the so-called Global South is increasing. In the weeks leading up to the UN General Assembly, the leaders of developing nations met at the BRICS summits in South Africa, the G20 in India, and the G77+China in Cuba.

For Brazil and the other countries of the Global South, the challenge is to maintain political independence and action, seeking to defend the interests of their populations, without taking sides in the dispute over the new global hegemony between China and the United States. It's the concept of active non-alignment.

Concluding his speech in New York, Lula recalled that "the UN needs to fulfil its role as a builder of a more just, supportive and fraternal world. But it will only do so if its members have the courage to proclaim their indignation at inequality and work tirelessly to overcome it".

Brazil and the Global South must endeavour to reform the multilateral system, such as the unsustainable composition of the Security Council, while respecting all its norms - especially with regard to the UN Charter and all human rights protection mechanisms, including the International Criminal Court. Only in this way will it be possible to reaffirm the legitimacy of multilateralism, reduce global power asymmetries and try to put out the fires that threaten our planet.

Viewpoint 2

> *"Countries at war sometimes target civilians to 'send messages' about the cost of challenging their narrative."*

The International Community Is Not Doing Enough to Protect Journalists and Aid Workers in Areas of Conflict

Chris Paterson

In this viewpoint Chris Paterson discusses the killings of journalists and aid workers in a number of conflicts, particularly in wars in the Middle East. The author discusses instances of this in the conflict in Gaza that began in 2023, but also the deaths of journalists caused by the U.S. military in Iraq and Afghanistan in the early 2000s. The UN promotes ensuring the safety of aid workers and journalists from warring parties, but this has largely been ignored. This suggests that civilians working to document conflict and offer aid to those impacted by conflict are being targeted and need better protection from the international community. Chris Paterson is a professor of global communication at the University of Leeds in the UK.

As you read, consider the following questions:

1. How is "deconfliction" defined in the viewpoint?

"Too Many Journalists and Aid Workers Are Being Killed in Gaza Despite Rules that Should Keep Them Safe," by Chris Paterson, The Conversation, April 30, 2024, https://theconversation.com/too-many-journalists-and-aid-workers-are-being-killed-in-gaza-despite-rules-that-should-keep-them-safe-227201.

2. When did the UN Security Council start promoting deconfliction?
3. According to data cited in this viewpoint, what percentage of journalists working in Gaza have been killed? How does this compare to other occupational groups?

Deconfliction" is a term familiar to anyone involved in wars around the world. It's an arrangement by which non-combatants, including aid workers and journalists, try to ensure their safety by informing warring parties of their movements to prevent themselves becoming targets.

We heard about deconfliction in the wake of the recent killing of seven humanitarian workers by the Israeli military. The organisation for which they were working, World Central Kitchen (WCK), insisted it had informed the Israel Defense Forces (IDF) of its workers' route as they collected aid supplies to deliver to depots for distribution.

Tragically, due to what Israel has called a "grave mistake", the convoy was hit and the seven humanitarian workers were killed in an airstrike that targeted vehicles bearing the WCK logo.

Deconfliction has clearly not been working well during Israel's assault on Gaza. On April 2, the UN secretary general, António Guterres, said 196 aid workers, including 175 from the UN, had been killed in Gaza. *The New York Times* has published a visual investigation describing six Israeli attacks on aid workers.

The concept of deconfliction—and its shortcomings—will be sadly familiar to journalists with experience of Middle East wars. I have been researching the safety of journalists since the early 2000s, when their deaths caused by the U.S. military in Iraq and Afghanistan became a regular occurrence.

Two decades ago, BBC journalist Nic Gowing, who went to Washington in an attempt to secure protection for media workers, wrote:

> There is a growing fear that some governments—especially the most militarily sophisticated, like the U.S. and Israel—are sanctioning the active targeting of journalists in war zones.

WCK's founder, José Andrés, told an Israeli broadcaster that this was "a direct attack on clearly marked vehicles whose movements were known by everybody at the IDF". Clearly, nothing has changed in two decades of conflict in the Middle East. But why not? Much of the news coverage of the WCK deaths has focused on why deconfliction hasn't worked. Let's examine the context.

The U.S. War on Terror Undermined Human Rights Accountability

The Special Rapporteur on Extrajudicial, Summary or Arbitrary Executions issued the following statement today:

"In recent years the United States has consistently argued that the UN Human Rights Council, and all other international human rights accountability mechanisms, have no legitimate role to play when individuals are intentionally killed, so long as it is claimed that the actions were part of the 'war on terror'," says Philip Alston, the United Nations Special Rapporteur on extrajudicial, summary or arbitrary executions. "While this argument is convenient because it enables the U.S. to effectively exempt itself from scrutiny, if accepted it would constitute a huge step backwards in the struggle to promote human rights. The argument would mean, for example, that the UN Human Rights Council would have no role to play in many of the most chronic situations of human rights violations around the world. All that would be needed is for the governments concerned to invoke the existence of an armed conflict in order to rid themselves of any human rights accountability."

Alston's concerns arose out of the U.S. Government's response to a letter he wrote on 26 August 2005, seeking an official response to information he had received that Haitham al-Yemeni had been

Targeting Journalists

The UN security council has promoted the deconfliction process to UN member states since 2016. It was instituted by the UN in 2018 to keep humanitarian workers in Yemen safe from attack by Saudi forces.

But there was already plenty of evidence that, for journalists at least, it offered little or no protection. When the U.S. moved into Afghanistan in 2001 and then Iraq in 2003, media organisations routinely used this approach. It often didn't work. In November

killed on the Pakistan-Afghanistan border in May 2005 by a missile fired by an un-manned aerial drone operated by the U.S. Central Intelligence Agency. Rather than accusing the United States of violating any law, Alston had instead sought "clarification" of the facts and of the Government's views on the legal issues involved.

The response of the U.S. Government was unprecedented "because it took the opportunity to challenge the entire international human rights system." The Government argued that international human rights law did not apply to the incident; that the laws that did apply could not be addressed by the Special Rapporteur or, implicitly, by the Human Rights Council; and that each State could determine for itself whether any particular incident could be addressed by the Council.

Alston responded with a 13-page letter critiquing the Government's position. "The incident involved was by no means the most alarming that I've dealt with this year, but the U.S. government is a key player and its use of an argument with very far-reaching negative implications for the system as a whole is especially troubling." says Alston.

"UN Expert on Extrajudicial Killings Tells United States War on Terror Could Undermine Human Rights Accountability," United Nations, March 28, 2007.

2001, journalists were injured as U.S. missiles hit both the BBCand Al Jazeera bureaus.

After interviewing a CIA official, U.S. investigative journalist Ron Suskind told me: "My sources are clear that that was done on purpose, precisely to send a message to Al Jazeera, and essentially a message was sent…There was great anger at Al Jazeera."

As U.S. forces entered Baghdad in April 2003, Al Jazeera correspondent Tareq Ayyoub was killed by a U.S. missile as he started a live broadcast from the roof of his bureau. The company had sent the Pentagon its coordinates and been assured the night before by the U.S. State Department that the bureau "was safe and would not be targeted".

Washington denied it had a responsibility to protect journalists, and warned news organisations that didn't "embed" with the U.S. military (putting their reporting under U.S. control) that they would be at risk. BBC correspondent Kate Adie told an Irish broadcaster in early 2003 that U.S. forces threatened to launch missiles at media transmitting from Baghdad.

A few hours after Ayoub's death, two more journalists were killed when a U.S. tank fired into the Palestine Hotel, which was housing the world's media. An Army analyst would later reveal the hotel was on a target list, and her efforts to tell superiors that it was full of journalists (whose calls she'd been monitoring) had been rebuffed.

My book about American attacks on the media traces the start of U.S. willingness to use violence against civilian reporters to the targeting of Yugoslav communication infrastructure in 1997—a means to control "the information space". In 1999, the infrastructure targeted was Serbia's public broadcaster, and NATO casually dismissed the deaths of 16 media personnel.

Israel's Track Record

Well before the Gaza invasion, press freedom groups documented hundreds of attacks on media by the Israeli military. A BBC driver in Lebanon was killed by an Israeli shell in 2000, and a British coroner's court found, in 2006, that documentary maker James Miller had been unlawfully killed by Israeli soldiers while working in Gaza.

A Reuters photographer was killed by an Israeli tank in Gaza in 2008, and in 2022, Palestinian-American Al Jazeera reporter Shireen Abu Akleh—despite reportedly wearing "press" identification was killed in Jenin by Israeli soldiers, in what numerous investigations deemed a deliberate act.

Even though foreign media have been kept out of Gaza by Israel, many residents there work for the media or report to global audiences online. The International Federation of journalists has estimated that since the hostilities began, the death toll of civilians has included "at least 109 journalists and media workers, a mortality rate of over 10 percent—dramatically higher than any other occupational group".

A month into the conflict, the leader of the local journalists' union pleaded for support. He described how the family of Al Jazeera correspondent Wael Al-Dahdouh were killed. Another died as an ambulance trying to save him came under attack.

Countries at war sometimes target civilians to "send messages" about the cost of challenging their narrative—and one Gaza journalist, Sami Abu Salem, has explained how persistent threats get in the way of reporting the situation there.

There are long-running campaigns to end the impunity of states who attack journalists, but humanitarian organizations need to be cautious to avoid antagonising militaries.

We must ask now if civilian organisations seeking to work in conflict zones need better protection than these ad-hoc deconfliction agreements—perhaps in the form of automatic sanction of combatants who break international humanitarian law.

Viewpoint 3

> *"Congress should codify a definition of transnational repression, and work with the executive branch and civil society to ensure laws offer protection against all of its varieties."*

The U.S. Must Establish a Stronger Policy Against Transnational Repression

Freedom House

Freedom House feels strongly that the alleged moral beacon of the world—the United States—has not done enough to halt or at least limit transnational repression on the world stage, particularly among the more repressive authoritarian regimes. It offers many suggestions in this viewpoint that the organization believes are necessary to allow America to take a stand against transnational repression while taking actual steps to curb its use. Preventing perpetrators from committing transnational repression and holding those who commit it accountable needs to be codified in law. Freedom House is a nonprofit organization that advocates for democracy, political freedom, and human rights.

As you read, consider the following questions:

1. Which U.S. government agencies does the author assert could help address the issue of transnational repression?

2. How does Freedom House suggest preventing perpetrators from committing transnational repression?
3. How do refugee resettlement programs factor into Freedom House's recommendations?

The recommendations listed below are intended to constrain the ability of states to commit acts of transnational repression, to increase accountability for perpetrators of transnational repression, and to provide protection for at-risk exiles and diasporas.

Reducing opportunities for authoritarian states to manipulate institutions within democracies will make it harder for them to target exiles and diasporas. Consistent accountability will moreover raise the cost of transnational repression for perpetrators.

Recommendations for Improving the United States' Response to Transnational Repression at Home and Abroad

Raising Awareness About the Threat of Transnational Repression

Ensure that law enforcement officials, personnel at key agencies, and those working with refugees are trained to recognize transnational repression. Law enforcement officials and agency personnel can play a central role in protecting exiles who are targeted. For example, timely diplomatic intervention, whether public or private, in isolation or in coordination with other states, can be the difference between an unlawful deportation and freedom for a targeted individual. Personnel at key agencies should receive training to help them identify potential perpetrators and victims of transnational repression, and on the relevant laws that can be invoked to combat transnational repression and mitigate harm. These key agencies include the Department of State; the Department of Homeland Security (DHS), including

U.S. Customs and Border Protection (CBP), U.S. Citizenship and Immigration Services (USCIS), and U.S. Immigration and Customs Enforcement (ICE); the Department of Justice, including the Federal Bureau of Investigation (FBI); other federal, state, and local law enforcement officials receiving instruction at the Federal Law Enforcement Training Center, and business and community leaders completing the Citizens Academy; and employees of the Department of Health and Human Service's Office of Refugee Resettlement (ORR). Training programs should be ongoing, taking place periodically across levels of seniority.

Ensure comprehensive reporting on transnational repression in State Department's Human Rights Reports. Since 2019, U.S. State Department Country Reports on Human Rights Practices have included a section on "politically motivated reprisals against individuals located outside the country." This section should be strengthened and made consistent across all country reports to help create a more robust record of transnational repression, encourage greater awareness of the phenomenon, and help officials better respond to the problem. A provision included in the FY23 National Defense Authorization Act (NDAA) requires the Departments of Justice and State to produce biannually a report detailing, among other things, "a list of countries that the Attorney General and the Secretary determine have repeatedly abused and misused the Red Notice and diffusion mechanisms for political purposes." The countries highlighted in this joint report and the details about their misuse of Interpol should be included in the relevant State Department Human Rights Reports.

Issue travel advisories about countries engaging in transnational repression. Potential targets of transnational repression are at particular risk when traveling abroad, and US citizens and residents have been targeted while outside of the United States. The U.S. Department of State provides travel advisories regarding issues abroad that may impact the safety and security of American travelers. This information, which typically includes details about terrorist and security threats, crime, civil unrest, and health and environmental risks, is intended to help U.S. citizens make informed decisions about whether or not to travel abroad. Advisories should be issued about countries whose governments engage in transnational repression or where acts of transnational repression frequently occur.

Establish standardized outreach procedures for vulnerable communities. In August 2021, the FBI began to issue unclassified counterintelligence bulletins describing the risks faced by Uyghurs and other diaspora groups from transnational repression. The bulletins contained information on specific incidents and directed individuals to contact the FBI if they had experienced targeting. In February 2022, the FBI launched a website devoted to transnational repression with information on tactics, hyperlinks to recent indictments, and contact information for reporting. The FBI should continue producing resources for vulnerable groups and publishing them in relevant languages. State and local law enforcement should conduct similar outreach as appropriate, and federal, state, and local law enforcement agencies should continue working jointly to investigate leads on suspected transnational repression in the United States. Many victims of transnational repression come from countries where law enforcement officials are involved in perpetrating abuses on behalf of the state, contributing to potential distrust of US law enforcement agents. Building trust with targeted communities is critical to addressing transnational repression threats before they escalate. Communities that understand how law enforcement can protect them, and that outreach to law enforcement will not result in negative consequences, are more resilient to foreign coercion and surveillance. To supplement these informational efforts, law enforcement should provide guidance to vulnerable communities on how to document evidence of harassment, intimidation, or stalking to help mitigate obstacles to reporting and prosecution. Law enforcement should consult with stakeholders including civil society and technology companies to develop and publicize this guidance. Other agencies, especially those working with migrants and refugees, should develop similar outreach strategies.

Congress should pass the bipartisan Foreign Advanced Technology Surveillance Accountability Act (H.R.2075) to better understand which governments use surveillance to target victims of transnational repression. This bill would require the Department of State to include information in its annual Human Rights Reports about the extent to which governments are using excessive surveillance or advanced technologies to violate rights. The report should also include information on which companies or countries have provided biometric or facial-recognition data to states using these technologies to violate rights. A more detailed understanding of which countries use surveillance to target critics can assist development of safeguards for potential victims of transnational repression, and of targeted sanctions for perpetrators.

Work with the Department of Justice and other relevant agencies to update transparency laws regarding individuals acting on behalf of foreign governments. A critical step in curbing transnational repression is recognizing the specific actors committing transnational abuses on behalf of their home governments. In the United States, antiquated procedures for regulation of foreign agents under the Foreign Agent Registrations Act of 1938 (22 U.S.C. 611 et seq) and 18 U.S.C. Section 951 are a major obstacle to identifying those acting on behalf of repressive regimes. Although the Department of Justice has ramped up enforcement against alleged perpetrators of transnational repression, the laws remain outdated and do not address the realities of modern-day foreign influence activities. The absence of effective regulation in this area makes it harder than it should be to distinguish legal activity on behalf of a foreign power or entity from illegal activity, and thus to address transnational repression threats before they escalate. Congress should closely consult civil society groups to mitigate unintended consequences in any update, such as U.S.-based organizations being required to register as foreign agents simply because they receive portions of their funding from non-U.S. sources.

Work at international organizations and bodies with like-minded governments to highlight the threat of transnational repression and establish international norms for addressing it. The United States should work with partners and allies to call for the creation of a special rapporteur for transnational repression at the United Nations. The United States should use its voice, vote, and influence to introduce resolutions at bodies to which it belongs condemning the use of transnational repression and calling on governments to bring accountability for abuses and protection for victims.

Limiting the Ability of Perpetrators to Commit Transnational Repression

Congress should codify a definition of transnational repression, and work with the executive branch and civil society to ensure laws offer protection against all of its varieties. Many types of transnational repression fall outside the scope of activities covered by existing law. This can make it more difficult for law enforcement agents to assist victims and apprehend and prosecute perpetrators. Codification of a definition of transnational repression is a needed first step toward determining which new authorities may be needed. A possible definition could include the following: "The term transnational repression describes the ways a government reaches across national borders to intimidate, silence, or harm an exile, refugee, or member of diaspora who they perceive as a threat and have a political incentive to control. Methods of transnational repression include assassinations, physical assaults, detention, rendition, unlawful deportation, unexplained or enforced disappearance, physical surveillance or stalking, passport cancellation or control over other documents, Interpol abuse, digital threats, spyware, cyberattacks, social media surveillance, online harassment, and harassment of or harm to family and associates who remain in the country of origin." Close attention should be given to the protection of civil liberties as new laws are considered.

Examine the domestic utility of and international experience with laws criminalizing "individual espionage." Spying on refugees, a common tactic of transnational repression, is not directly criminalized in the United States. In a number of Nordic and Western European countries, spying on individuals is either explicitly criminalized as "refugee espionage," or clearly incorporated into general espionage provisions. In the United States, however, espionage is narrowly defined as the collection or distribution of sensitive defense information. A new statute addressing "individual espionage" or similar activities might help law enforcement address transnational repression. Study of this issue should include any possible negative spillover effects for refugees and migrants themselves.

Create a screening process for diplomatic visas to prevent the entry or accreditation of diplomatic personnel with a history of harassing, intimidating, or harming their diasporas. Doing so could prevent transnational repression before it occurs. If diplomatic personnel already within the United States are found to be engaging in transnational repression, they should be designated personae non gratae and expelled, or held accountable under law when appropriate.

Give extra scrutiny to export licensing applications from companies exporting products to countries whose governments engage in human rights abuses, especially those previously identified as perpetrators of transnational repression. The United States, Australia, Denmark, and Norway, supported by Canada, France, the Netherlands, and the United Kingdom, recently announced the Export Controls and Human Rights Initiative, intended to "help stem the tide of authoritarian government misuse of technology and promote a positive vision for technologies anchored by democratic values." The United States also recently updated its licensing policy to restrict the export of items if there is "a risk that the items will be used to violate or abuse human rights." When implementing these new initiatives and policies, the United States should consult research by Freedom House and other human rights organizations to determine whether there is a risk that the exported items could enable human rights abuses. Extra scrutiny should be given to the export of items that could enable transnational repression, especially if those items are intended for countries whose governments have been identified as perpetrators of transnational repression.

Apply the voice, vote, and influence of the U.S. government to limit the ability of Interpol member countries to target critics through misuse of Red Notices and other alerts. Interpol's executive leadership includes representatives of governments notorious for perpetrating human rights abuses, including transnational repression. In November 2021, Ahmed Naser al-Raisi of the United Arab Emirates (UAE) was elected president of Interpol; he is the subject of lawsuits filed in the United Kingdom, Sweden, Norway, France, and Turkey accusing him of complicity in torture inside UAE's prisons. The UAE has also cooperated with other countries engaging in transnational repression and has engaged in transnational repression of its own. In that same election, Hu Binchen, deputy director general of the Chinese public security ministry, was elected to Interpol's executive committee. The government of China conducts the most sophisticated, global, and comprehensive campaign of transnational repression in the world. Al-Raisi and Hu join senior Interpol officials from Turkey and India, whose governments have also engaged in transnational repression. The United States is by far the largest statutory contributor to Interpol's budget and should leverage its contributions alongside other democracies to improve the functioning of Interpol, reduce opportunities for abuse, and support the candidacy of individuals for leadership positions who will enforce Interpol's commitment to human rights.

Prohibit the use of Interpol notices on their own to deny immigration or asylum benefits or conduct arrests. At present, ICE can and does use Interpol notices as proof of an immigration offence to invalidate an individual's legal visa and to challenge a claim for asylum. Though it is unclear how frequently this occurs each year, this practice leads to detention and the risk of deportation. To ensure perpetrators are not able to mislead agents of the U.S. government into aiding and abetting acts of transnational repression, law should require that notices issued by countries with which the U.S. does not have an extradition agreement be independently verified before they are applied against individuals in the U.S. on lawful visas or making a claim for asylum. Current Department of Justice policy prohibits the arrest of an individual solely on the basis of an Interpol Red Notice because these notices do not meet the probable cause standard of the Constitution. This policy should be codified.

The Department of Homeland Security's Office of Inspector General should investigate the extent to which Interpol notices are used to invalidates visas or as probable cause to believe that a person applying for asylum has committed a serious nonpolitical crime. The report should include detailed information on the number of incidents where ICE or DHS use Interpol notices as evidence against a noncitizen in the United States, the countries that issued the notices that were used, the claims included in those notices, whether any of the cases would count as transnational repression, and detailed recommendations for ensuring that U.S. immigration officials and judges are not unwittingly complicit in acts of transnational repression.

Bringing Accountability for Acts of Transnational Repression

Deploy a robust strategy for targeted sanctions against perpetrators of transnational repression. Targeted sanctions, such as denying or revoking visas for entry to the United States, or freezing U.S.-based assets, enjoy broad bipartisan support and should play a key role in raising the cost of transnational repression for perpetrators. To make sanctions as impactful as possible:

- Impose the strongest possible targeted sanctions on perpetrators and enablers of acts of transnational repression. Current law and presidential actions allow for targeted sanctions on individuals (including both government officials and private citizens) and entities involved in human rights abuses, including assassinations and renditions, which are some of the most serious forms of transnational repression. In some cases, the family members of perpetrators are also eligible for sanction.
- Impose export controls on companies that knowingly provided technologies, goods, or services to facilitate the commission of transnational repression. Policymakers should investigate the extent to which commercial surveillance tools, such as spyware and extraction technology, have been used against Americans and in the commission of transnational repression.

- Congress should pass the Revealing and Explaining Exclusions for Accountability (REVEAL) Act (S.2392/H.R.4557). Section 212(a)(3)(C) of the Immigration and Nationality Act (INA) allows the U.S. government to deny entry to a person if there is "reasonable ground to believe [that person's entry to the United States] would have potentially serious adverse foreign policy consequences." But, under current law the names of those denied entry and reasons for their denial may not be made public. The REVEAL Act would allow names and reasons for visa denial to be made public—a naming and shaming tactic that could help deter future abuses.
- Congress and the executive branch should work together to ensure robust funding for the implementation and enforcement of targeted sanctions. The U.S. Department of the Treasury, Department of State, and Department of Justice all collect information about suspected perpetrators of abuses eligible for sanction. Unfortunately, the number of potential sanctions cases to be vetted by the U.S. government far exceeds current capacity, and the recent flurry of sanctions related to the Kremlin's invasion of Ukraine has added to this workload. Funding for additional personnel in relevant sanctions offices would help ensure the executive branch has adequate capacity to implement sanctions policies.

Restrict security assistance for states engaging in transnational repression. Section 502B of the Foreign Assistance Act of 1961, as amended (22 USC 2304), is intended to "promote and encourage respect for human rights and fundamental freedoms throughout the world" by making the observance of human rights a "principal goal of U.S. foreign policy." Current law prohibits the provision of security assistance to any government engaging "in a consistent pattern of gross violations of internationally recognized human rights" unless the president certifies to Congress that "extraordinary circumstances" warrant the provision of assistance. This section should be updated to allow the restriction of security assistance for states consistently engaging in acts of transnational repression. This would serve the dual purpose of limiting an aggressor government's resources for engaging in transnational repression while also sending a strong signal that the behavior is unacceptable.

Supporting Victims of Transnational Repression

Ensure the United States maintains a robust refugee resettlement program and an efficient, rights-based approach to assessing claims for asylum to protect victims of transnational repression and others fleeing persecution. As Congress noted in the Refugee Resettlement Act of 1980, "it is the historic policy of the United States to respond to the urgent needs of persons subject to persecution in their homelands." Many refugees fled political persecution in countries that engage in transnational repression, and face threats even after resettlement. Refugees who live in strong democracies where the rule of law is upheld and institutions are accountable have stronger basic protection against transnational repression than those who do not. With this in mind, the Biden administration should commit to rebuilding the country's refugee resettlement program and provide adequate resources to eliminate the asylum processing backlog. Each year, the president and Congress work together to set an annual cap on the number of allowable refugee resettlement admissions for that year. Historically, the cap has been as high as 207,116 in 1980, and as low as 15,000 in 2021. The Biden administration should work with Congress to uphold the United States' commitment to refugee resettlement and ensure that victims of transnational repression have the chance to enter the United States as refugees. Victims of transnational repression who are already in the United States and seeking asylum face a years-long wait due to a claims processing backlog and are especially vulnerable while their legal status remains in limbo. Asylum seekers cannot reunite with their families abroad, face delays securing eligibility for employment, are unable to pursue educational opportunities, and face the threat of deportation. As of the end of the fiscal year 2021, USCIS had 412,796 pending applications for asylum.

Viewpoint 4

> *"Both the ICJ and the ICC are international judicial institutions located in the Hague. Both courts are a significant part of the international legal infrastructure aiming to consolidate and promote the international rule of law."*

Can International Courts Help Address Transnational Repression?

Avidan Kent, Kirsten McConnachie, and Rishi Gulati

In this viewpoint Avidan Kent, Kirsten McConnachie, and Rishi Gulati explain the two international courts that promote international rule of law: the International Court of Justice (ICJ) and the International Criminal Court (ICC). They explain that the ICJ is a part of the UN, while the ICC is an independent international organization. The ICC establishes individual criminal responsibility for international crimes and depends on states to comply with arrest warrants. The ICJ is focused on state responsibility rather than individual responsibility for these crimes and can order reparations be paid, but it depends on the cooperation of both parties involved in conflict. Both courts can play an important role in shaping international opinion about countries who commit crimes against humanity like transnational

"What Are the ICJ and the ICC and How Do Their Power and Jurisdiction Differ?," by Avidan Kent, Kirsten McConnachie, and Rishi Gulati, The Conversation, May 22, 2024, https://theconversation.com/what-are-the-icj-and-the-icc-and-how-do-their-power-and-jurisdiction-differ-230573.

repression and extrajudicial killings. Avidan Kent is a senior lecturer in law at the University of East Anglia in the UK, where Kirsten McConnachie is a professor of socio-legal studies and Rishi Gulati is an associate professor in international law.

As you read, consider the following questions:

1. What different approaches are the ICJ and ICC taking to the conflict in Gaza based on their jurisdictions?
2. What are ICJ advisory opinions?
3. Why did U.S. Secretary of State Antony Blinken claim the ICC has no jurisdiction to issue arrest warrants for the conflict in Gaza?

The international court of justice (ICJ) and the international criminal court (ICC) have been heavily involved in the politicking surrounding the conflict in Gaza. As the ICJ hears arguments surrounding accusations of genocide levelled at Israel, the ICC prosecutor recently applied for arrest warrants to be issued for the leaders both of the state of Israel and the Hamas militant group, which are engaged in bitter and deadly conflict in the Palestinian enclave.

Both the ICJ and the ICC are international judicial institutions located in the Hague. Both courts are a significant part of the international legal infrastructure aiming to consolidate and promote the international rule of law.

But it is important to appreciate that the ICJ and ICC are different bodies that perform distinct functions. The ICJ is the principal judicial organ of the United Nations (UN). It was established in 1945 by the United Nations charter, and it consists of 15 judges elected by the UN general assembly and the security council.

On the other hand, established in 2001, the ICC is an independent international organisation that was created by a treaty called the Rome Statute. It is the first permanent, treaty-based, international criminal court created to help end impunity for the perpetrators of the most serious of international crimes.

Operation and Powers

The ICC is a criminal court that seeks to establish individual criminal responsibility for the most serious international crimes. It has a prosecutor with the power to carry out investigations of crimes within the jurisdiction of the ICC and the court can issue arrest warrants for individuals believed to have committed those crimes.

The ICC does not have a police force but state parties are obliged to comply with a requested arrest warrant. Trials are conducted as a criminal trial (with prosecution and defence counsel) before a tribunal of judges. The ICC can impose prison sentences, order fines and seizure of assets derived from the crimes committed. It also has the power to issue reparations to victims. It cannot impose the death penalty.

The ICJ, meanwhile, is concerned with state responsibility rather than individual culpability. A judgment of the ICJ can determine whether a state party to the case has breached international law and order reparations (including guarantees of non-repetition as well as financial compensation or restitution) for such a breach.

It will not identify individual perpetrators or assign individual responsibility. If a state believes there are rights in immediate danger, it can request the ICJ to issue "provisional measures" to preserve those rights until the case proceedings are completed. For example, provisional measures were requested and ordered in the case of South Africa v. Israel to prevent continued alleged violations of the genocide convention.

Jurisdiction

The ICJ is a general court for the settlement of disputes between states and can accept disputes regarding any question of international law, including such issues as border disputes, diplomatic immunity, environmental protection, genocide and more. The ICC, in contrast, is a criminal court with jurisdiction limited only to the four crimes listed in the Rome Statute: genocide, crimes against humanity, war crimes, and aggression.

While the ICJ can in principle deal with cases brought by any state, the ICC's jurisdiction is more limited. It covers crimes that were committed in the territory of, or by the nationals of, one of the 124 member states of the Rome Statute.

Countries such as the U.S., China, Russia, and Israel are not parties to the Rome Statute, hence the reported view by the U.S. secretary of state, Antony Blinken, that the ICC has no jurisdiction when it comes to issuing arrest warrants over the conflict in Gaza.

Beyond these limitations, the ICC can deal with crimes conducted anywhere in the world, should the UN security council ask it to do so.

How Do Cases Come Before the Two Courts?

ICJ cases come before the court only with the disputing states' consent. In other words, states cannot be "dragged" to court. A recent example is South Africa v. Israel. Israel provided consent to resolve disputes that are related to the genocide convention before the ICJ when it signed the treaty in 1950, agreeing to take part in this legal process.

ICJ decisions in contentious proceedings are binding on the parties, although the court is unable to enforce its decisions.

A second type of ICJ cases are called "advisory opinions". These are not traditional cases, so they are not legally binding, and they do not involve traditional "parties" to a dispute. Rather, this process permits a list of international organisations to send questions to the ICJ concerning international law, which the ICJ will answer by writing a legal opinion. While not legally binding, these legal opinions are regarded as authoritative and are often followed by states.

The ICJ was asked in the past to provide advisory opinions on a range of issues such as the legality of nuclear weapons, the independence of Kosovo, and lately also the obligations of states with respect to climate change.

ICC cases are initiated differently. Any of the 124 member states of the Rome Statute can refer a situation to the court, asking the prosecutor—currently UK barrister Karim Khan KC—to conduct a preliminary investigation. Alternatively, the UN security council can refer a case to the ICC, as was done, for example, concerning the situation in Darfur.

Finally, the ICC prosecutor has the authority to launch an investigation on his own initiative. Which in the case of the conflict in Gaza, he has done—hence his application for international arrest warrants issued on May 20.

Viewpoint 5

> *"Since the 1950s, nearly 90 percent of the U.S. penalties that have proved to be effective were imposed on states with multiparty electoral systems—most of which are democracies. In fact, sanctions against dictatorships rarely meet the three necessary criteria for sanctions to work."*

Why Sanctions Don't Work Against Dictatorships

Agathe Demarais

In this viewpoint Agathe Demarais expresses what many around the world have thought—that sanctions against authoritarian countries remain ineffective. The viewpoint goes on to provide ample proof backing up this assertion and tries to explain why they do not have their desired effect. But are there any peaceful alternatives to sanctions? Democratic world leaders might not feel that there are any other methods of punishment that would not threaten to heighten tensions or even lead to a dangerous conflict. Agathe Demarais is global forecasting director of the Economist Intelligence Unit at the Journal of Democracy *and the author of* Backfire: How Sanctions Reshape the World Against U.S. Interests.

As you read, consider the following questions:

1. Which kinds of sanctions tend to work, according to this viewpoint?
2. According to the author, how can sanctions backfire on the world stage?
3. Despite being imperfect, why does Demarais think sanctions are important?

Within hours of Vladimir Putin's order to invade Ukraine on 24 February 2022, Western governments imposed far-reaching sanctions on Russia. The United States and the European Union placed embargos on hydrocarbon imports, froze part of the Kremlin's foreign-exchange reserves, and disconnected dozens of Russian banks from the international financial system—a vise that continues to tighten to this day. But more than eight months later, Putin has not backed down despite devastating blows to Russia's economy. Have sanctions missed their target?

Over the past two decades, Western democracies have made sanctions their go-to diplomatic weapon. The United States and European Union administer hundreds of sanctions programs, targeting thousands of individuals, companies, and economic sectors in nearly every single country. But there may be a catch when it comes to sanctioning an authoritarian power such as Russia: Sanctions seem to work best against democracies. Since the 1950s, nearly 90 percent of the U.S. penalties that have proved to be effective were imposed on states with multiparty electoral systems—most of which are democracies. In fact, sanctions against dictatorships rarely meet the three necessary criteria for sanctions to work.

What Works

First, effective sanctions typically have a narrowly defined objective. In 2018, the United States slapped sanctions on Turkey to protest the detention of Andrew Brunson, an American pastor, who allegedly had links to groups that the Turkish government deems "terrorists." (He denied those allegations.) Just two months later, Turkey bowed to this pressure and released him, prompting the United States to lift the related penalties. While Turkey isn't a democracy, it isn't a full-blown autocracy either.

By contrast, sanctions against dictatorships, such as those long imposed on Cuba and North Korea, often have broad objectives—namely, regime change. International penalties with the aim of toppling governments almost always fail: The leaders of Cuba and North Korea have no intention of caving to pressure because giving up power means signing their own arrest (or death) warrants. Moreover, international penalties against authoritarian regimes rarely hurt ruling elites. Despite a heap of UN and Western sanctions, members of North Korea's elite still have access to luxury goods thanks to the smuggling networks the country has built to evade them. In fact, the United Nations estimates that Kim Jong Un's luxury-goods expenses top $US600 million annually.

Media censorship—the hallmark of dictatorships—means that sanctioned countries can pretend that sanctions are the sole cause of economic hardship even when their own economic policies are at fault. Venezuela is a textbook example. Years of economic mismanagement have brought about a deep economic crisis, but the country's rulers have found a perfect scapegoat in sanctions. As a result, 60 percent of Venezuelans oppose sanctions and blame those who have imposed them for their economic hardship. In fact, the recent rise in popularity of President Nicolás Maduro may have been due to his opponent Juan Guaidó's support of sanctions.

Second, sanctions are usually more effective if the country imposing them has significant economic ties to the targeted state. The 2018 U.S. sanctions against Turkey worked partly for this reason: The two countries have significant economic links and are NATO allies. Sanctions were an extraordinary measure given these ties, and Turkey quickly accepted U.S. demands. Conversely, if Western states target a country with which they have few ties (as is the case with most dictatorships), then the targeted country will have little incentive to alter its behavior.

This explains why the most effective sanctions are multilateral ones. When many countries impose the same restrictions, targeted states are left with limited options to continue trading. Take the bevy of penalties that were imposed on Libya in the 1980s. At the time, the United States slapped sanctions on Libya for its support of several international terrorist attacks. These were not a problem for the regime of Muammar al-Qadhafi; he merely shifted Libya's oil exports toward Europe. He backed down only after sanctions garnered global support and the UN Security Council passed a resolution imposing penalties on Libya. Similar UN sanctions against Russia are impossible: The country holds a veto on the Security Council and has the support of China and many developing countries.

Third, many sanctions are designed to impose hardship on the populations of targeted countries so that they pressure their governments to change course. These sorts of penalties don't tend to work against authoritarian states: Citizens living under dictatorship have few means of persuading their rulers to change direction. Iran's experience from 2012 to 2015 is instructive. Western countries, wanting to force Iran to abandon its nuclear ambitions, imposed crippling sanctions—leading to the country's economic collapse, a sinking currency, and record inflation. Iranians resented the impact of Western sanctions, especially as the country had previously enjoyed decent living conditions.

Crucially, Iranian citizens had a way to signal their displeasure to their rulers. Iran is a theocracy with a dismal human-rights record, but still holds elections. In 2013, Iranians elected reformist Hassan Rouhani as president, tasking him with getting sanctions lifted. He delivered in 2015, signing the nuclear deal, which imposed limits on Iran's nuclear program in exchange for sanctions relief. But in countries where decision-making is wholly centralized, public pressure can fail to bring even a shift in policy direction.

Beyond their limited effectiveness, sanctions against dictatorships may well backfire on the international stage. A growing number of autocrats are using sanctions to foment anti-Western sentiment globally. After the invasion of Ukraine led to disruptions in wheat production and exports, the Kremlin's propagandists falsely blamed Western sanctions for rising global food insecurity. But the difficulties that Russia and Ukraine, two of the world's largest wheat producers, faced in exporting grain had nothing to do with sanctions; they were due to Russia's blockade of Ukrainian ports and Ukraine's (understandable) defensive mining of its waters. Yet this false narrative has gained traction, especially in poorer African and Middle Eastern countries.

Such anti-sanctions propaganda aims to foster resentment against Western states and democracy more broadly. To counter it, sanctioning countries must start mounting information campaigns explaining the rationale, mechanisms, and objectives of their penalties. If democracies fail to do so, both authoritarian regimes and extremist political parties at home will blame sanctions for the ills facing their societies. Europe is a case in point: Right-wing parties are claiming that international penalties on Russia are responsible for high inflation and the energy crisis—a message that the Kremlin has been all too happy to amplify. In fact, these problems are due to Russia's invasion of Ukraine and its weaponization of energy supplies.

The Best of the Worst

There is no shortage of evidence that sanctions against dictatorships are an imperfect tool at best. As such, sanctions against Russia are unlikely to persuade the Kremlin to change course in Ukraine. But that does not mean that Western governments should abandon them. In the absence of other viable options, sanctions still serve a purpose. They send a strong message, filling the gap between empty diplomatic declarations and deadly military interventions. While they may not persuade dictators to change course, they still circumscribe autocrats' abilities to achieve their goals or wage war against their neighbors.

Moreover, the debate over the effectiveness of sanctions often fails to recognize a crucial fact: The impact of sanctions is gradual and cumulative. This is especially the case for Western sanctions on Russia. Western penalties curb Russia's access to the financing and technology it needs to keep its energy sector thriving into the long term. Existing Russian energy fields are fast depleting, and if energy companies lack the resources to develop new ones, the Russian economy will slowly grind to a halt. In addition, the United States could still impose secondary sanctions on Russian oil exports, preventing other countries from buying Russia's crude. As such, sanctions signal to Putin that continuing to wage war against Ukraine will eventually result in the asphyxiation of the Russian economy.

Finally, no one knows what would have happened if sanctions had not been put into place. Perhaps things would be even worse in that alternative reality. Unconstrained, would Putin have chosen an even more ruthless strategy in Ukraine or decided to invade other East European countries? Only Putin knows. To paraphrase Winston Churchill, sanctions may be the worst form of diplomatic weapon, except for all the others that have been tried.

Periodical and Internet Sources Bibliography

The following articles have been selected to supplement the diverse views presented in this chapter.

"Declaration of Principles to Combat Transnational Repression," Freedom House Summit for Democracy, 2023. https://freedomhouse.org/2023/summit-for-democracy-transnational-repression.

"14-Point Program For the Prevention of Extrajudicial Executions," Amnesty International. https://www.amnesty.org/en/wp-content/uploads/2021/06/pol350021993en.pdf.

"Sikh Coalition Rallies Allies to Oppose Transnational Repression," Sikh Coalition, April 5, 2024. https://www.sikhcoalition.org/blog/2024/sikh-coalition-rallies-allies-to-oppose-transnational-repression/.

"Transnational Repression: A Global Problem," World Without Genocide. https://worldwithoutgenocide.org/genocides-and-conflicts/transnational-repression-a-global-problem.

Johannes Blad, "Economic Sanctions and Repression," Department of Peace and Conflict Research, Uppsala University, January 2019. https://www.diva-portal.org/smash/get/diva2:1277611/FULLTEXT01.pdf.

Ben Cardin, "Cardin, Merkley, Rubio, Hagerty Take a Stand Against Foreign Governments Trampling Human Rights Within the United States," U.S. Senate, March 16, 2023. https://www.cardin.senate.gov/press-releases/cardin-merkley-rubio-hagerty-take-a-stand-against-foreign-governments-trampling-human-rights-within-the-united-states/.

Sinjae Kang, Sangmin Lee, and Taehee Whang, "Economic Sanctions, Repression Capacity, and Human Rights," *Yonsei University Journal of Human Rights*, 2023. https://www.tandfonline.com/doi/full/10.1080/14754835.2022.2096404.

Reed M. Wood, "A Hand Upon the Throat of the Nation: Economic Sanctions and State Repression, 1976-2001," *International Studies Quarterly*, September 2008. https://www.jstor.org/stable/29734248.

Further Discussion

Chapter 1

1. Based on what you've read in this chapter, are the democracies of the world directly or indirectly responsible for transnational repression? Are they blameless? Use evidence from the viewpoints to explain your reasoning.
2. How has social media played a role in the proliferation of transnational repression?
3. Why do authoritarian regimes feel the need to repress dissidents outside their borders?

Chapter 2

1. When can military intervention in foreign wars be categorized as transnational repression or extrajudicial killing? Provide examples to support your argument.
2. According to viewpoints in this chapter, which human rights should be considered universal? Which rights discussed are violated by transnational repression and extrajudicial killing?
3. Based on what you've read in the viewpoints in this chapter, do you think the U.S.'s involvement in certain international conflicts counts as transnational repression? Why or why not?

Chapter 3

1. What is the moral difference—if any—between extrajudicial killing such as that of Jamal Khashoggi and targeted killings committed by the U.S. military against suspected terrorists? Explain your reasoning.
2. Did the lynching of African Americans and murder of Native Americans in the 1800s fall under the umbrella of extrajudicial killings? Was there a difference between the

two because the government was more involved in the latter? Explain your reasoning.
3. Should the United States have severed relations with Saudi Arabia after the Khashoggi killing? Why or why not?

Chapter 4

1. Is it possible for the United Nations, ICC, and ICJ to wield enough power to halt or limit transnational repression and extrajudicial killing?
2. According to the viewpoint by Agathe Demarais, why are sanctions considered too weak a response to transnational repression? Do you think there are any possible alternatives?
3. Based on what you've read in this chapter, what can the U.S., other Western democracies, and international bodies like the UN do to prevent and punish transnational repression and extrajudicial killing?

Organizations to Contact

The editors have compiled the following list of organizations concerned with the issues debated in this book. The descriptions are derived from materials provided by the organizations. All have publications or information available for interested readers. The list was compiled on the date of publication of the present volume; the information provided here may change. Be aware that many organizations take several weeks or longer to respond to inquiries, so allow as much time as possible.

Amnesty International

Calle Luz Savinon 519 Colonia del Valle
Benito Juarez 03100
Mexico City, Mexico
website: amnesty.org

This global organization consisting of more than 10 million people works toward human rights for everyone. It is an independent group unaffiliated with any religion or ideology. It stands for human rights victims and against government violators anywhere in the world.

Center for Victims of Torture

2356 University Avenue West, Suite 430
St. Paul, MN 55114
(612) 436-4800
email: cvtT@cvt.org
website: cvt.org

The mission of the Center for Victims of Torture is to heal the wounds of torture victims, their families, and communities. Its goal is to end torture worldwide by destroying barriers to justice and advocating for opportunities for everyone.

Committee To Protect Journalists

John S. and James L. Knight Foundation Press Freedom Center
PO Box 2675
New York, NY 10108
(212) 465-1004
website: cpj.org

The Committee to Protect Journalists is an independent, non-profit organization that promotes press freedom worldwide. It defends the right of journalists to report the news safely and without fear of reprisals. It protects the free flow of news and commentary by taking action wherever journalists are under threat.

Freedom House

1850 M St. NW
Washington, DC 20036
(202) 296-5101
email: info@freedomhouse.org
website: freedomhouse.org

Freedom House was founded on the core conviction that freedom flourishes in democratic nations where governments are accountable to their people. Its key issues are countering authoritarianism, promoting a global democratic landscape, and supporting defenders of democratic change.

Human Rights Institute (HRI)

600 New Jersey Avenue NW
Washington, DC 20001
(202) 662-9000
website: law.georgetown.edu/human-rights-institute/

The HRI is the focal point of human rights at the Georgetown University Law Center. It is a training ground for human rights advocates. The organization provides academic and real-world experience along with the practical skills needed to make a difference in helping further human rights in the United States and worldwide.

Human Rights Watch

350 Fifth Avenue, 34th Floor
New York, NY 10118-3299
(202) 290-4700
website: hrw.org

This organization investigates and reports on human rights abuses throughout the world. It consists of nation experts that includes lawyers and journalists from 70 different countries who seek to protect at-risk people, minorities, and civilians in war-torn areas, as well as refugees and children in need. It advocates toward governments and armed groups.

International Justice Mission (IJM)

PO Box 2227
Arlington, VA 22202
(844) 522-5878
website: ijm.org

IJM partners with justice systems throughout the world to build safe communities that are protected from violence and slavery. It seeks protection for those threatened and to bring criminals to justice.

Refugees International

1800 M Street NW, Suite 405N
Washington, DC 20036
(202) 828-0110
email: ri@refugeesinternational.org
website: refugeesinternational.org

Refugees International fights for the rights of refugees by working with its global partners to investigate challenges faced by displaced people, develop policy solutions, mobilize action, and punish violators. It is dedicated to expanding the space for refugee and local leadership in the public sphere and halls of power.

Sikh Coalition

165 Broadway 23rd Floor Office 2359
New York, N.Y. 10006
(212) 655-3095
email: resources@sikhcoalition.org
website: sikhcoalition.org

The goal of the Sikh Coalition is to protect the constitutional rights to practice faith without fear through the community, courtroom, classroom, and legislators. It is engaged in work against transnational repression in order to protect the civil rights and lives of U.S.-based Sikhs.

United States Government Accountability Office

441 G Street NW
Washington D.C. 20548
(202) 512-3000
email: contact@gao.gov
website: gao.gov

This self-described independent, non-partisan congressional watchdog seeks to ensure that taxpayer money is well spent and provides Congress and federal agencies work objectively and more efficiently. It is the supreme audit institution of the U.S. federal government.

Bibliography of Books

Sean Byrnes. *Disunited Nations: U.S. Foreign Policy, Anti-Americanism, and the Rise of the New Right*. Baton Rouge, LA: LSU Press, 2021.

Miriam J.A. Chancy. *Autochthonomies: Transnationalism, Testimony, and Transmission in the African Diaspora*. Champaign, IL: University of Illinois Press, 2020.

Patrice Cullors and Asha Bandele. *When They Call You a Terrorist: A Black Lives Matter Memoir*. New York, NY: St. Martin's Press, 2018.

Leah Hunt-Hendrix and Astra Taylor. *Solidarity: The Past, Present and Future of a World-Changing Idea*. New York: Pantheon Publishing, 2024.

Adam LeBor. *"Complicity with Evil": The United Nations in the Age of Modern Genocide*. New Haven, CT: Yale University Press, 2008.

Francesca Lessa. *The Condor Trials: Transnational Repression and Human Rights in South America*. New Haven, CT: Yale University Press, 2022.

Michael Lutterschmidt. *Extrajudicial Execution: The Dying Testimony of Michael James Lutterschmidt*. Edina, MN: Wisdom Editions, 2023.

Dana Moss and Saipira Furstenberg. *Transnational Repression in the Age of Globalism*. Edinburgh, UK: Edinburgh University Press, 2024.

Eva Pils. *Human Rights in China: A Social Practice in the Shadows of Authoritarianism*. Queensland, Australia: Polity Publishing, 2017.

Jonathan Rugman. *The Killing in the Consulate: The Life and Death of Jamal Khashoggi*. London, UK: Simon & Schuster UK, 2019.

Sayragul Sauytbay, Alexandra Cavelius, and Caroline Waight. *The Chief Witness: Escape From China's Modern-Day Concentration Camps*. Melbourne, Australia: Scribe, 2021.

W. Cleon Skousen. *The Naked Communist: Exposing Communism and Restoring Freedom*. Salt Lake City, UT: Izzard Ink Publishing, 2014.

Mac Taylor. *The Assault on Freedom in America*. Water Springs, FL: EABooks Publishing, 2018.

Ferhat Ünlü, Abdurrahman Şimşek, and Nazif Karaman. *Diplomatic Savagery: Dark Secrets Behind the Jamal Khashoggi Murder*. New York, NY: The Ishmael Tree, 2019.

Owen Wilson. *Murder in Istanbul: Jamal Khashoggi, Donald Trump and Saudi Arabia*. London, UK: Gibson Square Books, 2019.

Index

A

B

C

D

E

F

G

H

I

J

K

L

M

N

O

P

R

S

T

U

V

W

Y